The
Grazier's Proposal

Carolyn J. Pollack

The Grazier's Proposal

Copyright © 2022 by Carolyn J. Pollack.

Paperback ISBN: 978-1-63812-121-3
Ebook ISBN: 978-1-63812-122-0

All rights reserved. No part in this book may be produced and transmitted in any form or by any means, electronic, or mechanical, including photocopying, recording, or by any information storage and retrieval system, without permission in writing from the copyright owner.

The views expressed in this work are solely those of the author and do not necessarily reflect the views of the publisher hereby disclaims any responsibility for them.

Published by Pen Culture Solutions   02/16/2022

Pen Culture Solutions
1-888-727-7204 (USA)
1-800-950-458 (Australia)
support@penculturesolutions.com

Acknowledgements

I would like to acknowledge a special thank you to my fourth son, Christopher Allan Pollack, who graciously allowed me to use his image on the front cover of *The Grazier's Proposal*.

Also, thank you to his lovely partner, Skye McMillan for taking the photos for the front/back cover.

Chapter One

PETA SAT WATCHING DESPONDENTLY from the safety of her car as the rain fell steadily, saturating the surrounding landscape. The heavens had opened up, putting on a spectacular display which showed not a sign of abating any time soon.

"Great," she muttered sombrely. "What am I supposed to do now!" There was no way she was going to get out of her warm, dry car to fix a puncture in this torrential downpour.

Biting her lower lip indecisively, she considered her limited options, knowing there was really only one course of action to take, but she didn't relish the drenching that option gave her. She realised if she stayed in her car and waited for the rain to stop before fixing the puncture; she risked being stuck here on the side of the highway until well after dark.

With several hours of her journey still left to drive, the thought of spending the night alone in her car on the now semi deserted Capricorn Highway didn't fill her with enthusiasm. An icy shiver assaulted her senses as she realised she really only had one course of action open to her. Looking out at the bleak terrain through a mist shrouded windscreen, Peta could see the rain was coming down even harder than before. The sky was a deep leaden gray, letting her know in no uncertain terms the rain wasn't going to stop. If anything, there seemed to be the added promise of more rain to come.

Peta's mind returned to a conversation she'd overheard while getting petrol at her last rest stop. Two locals had been conversing about the approaching dark clouds and had been speculating on the amount of rain which would be dropped over the district. They'd been in total agreement that they were due for some good earth soaking rain, and both men had seemed confident that these storm clouds would break the dry spell which had held the land captive for the past few months. Peta was now forced to agree with them, for it seemed that the wet weather had definitely set in with a vengeance. She didn't begrudge the local landowners the rain, but she wished that she'd been able to outrun the downpour before her car had blown a tyre, leaving her stranded by the side of the road.

Next time she saw Nelson, she vowed she was going to give him the ear bashing of his life. One he richly deserved, she added for good measure. She blamed him completely for the predicament she found herself in.

Dear sweet Nelson. He was probably her best friend in the entire world, but if she was to set eyes on him at the moment, his life wouldn't be worth a grain of salt. She'd already tried to phone him, but there was no service. Whether that was because of the rain or where she was, she wasn't sure. And, she thought to herself crossly, I'm also going to insist that he keep the darn thing turned on. He had a bad habit of turning it off when he was away, saying that most of the places he had to visit had little or no service, so why waste his phone's battery.

Smiling ruefully to herself, Peta's thoughts returned to the chain of events surrounding the last twenty-four hours that now saw her stranded and alone by the side of the road. She'd been on a whirlwind buying trip to Brisbane, purchasing stock for her Arts and Craft shop in Rockhampton. An eight hour leisurely drive north on the Bruce Highway would have seen her safely home, but that was before she had contacted her lifelong friend, Nelson Young, telling him she was calling in for a quick cup of coffee before starting her journey home. A trip to Brisbane wouldn't be complete without a stop-over at Nelson's place. They'd been friends forever, since kindergarten, in fact.

Nelson and Helen had been delighted to see her and had ushered her into the lounge room of their spacious Mt. Cootha home.

"Jupiter, how wonderful to see you. Come in, come in," Nelson had told her warmly.

Peta gritted her teeth at Nelson's full use of her name, but she said nothing. He insisted on using it and she had grown used to it over the years, but she still didn't have to like it.

"So how did the buying trip for the shop go?" Helen asked, and the two women launched into a conversation of how the shop was going.

Nelson interrupted them a short time later by asking, "How would you like some company on your long, lonely drive back to Rockhampton?"

"I don't know," Peta responded jauntily. "How would I like it?"

"You'd love it." he told her just as sprightly, "especially since we'd be taking an alternative route."

"An alternative route . . . and just where is this alternative route going to take us?" she wanted to know. Falling in with one of Nelson's plans could see her going anywhere, and she really had to get home. She'd closed the shop for two days to come on this trip. She didn't want to be away any longer than she could help it. Nelson was a troubleshooter for a large firm based in Brisbane. The company manufactured farming equipment. It was his job to settle disputes, and to soothe away any complaints that might arise between the customer and the firm. His flamboyant personality made him perfect for this type of employment. He had a knack for being able to diffuse even the most adverse situation, whereby all parties were satisfied with the final outcome. "I have to go to Tambo . . . ,"

"Where," Peta interrupted, knowing if she didn't she wouldn't get the chance to inquire later, for some of Nelson's explanations could go on forever.

"Tambo," Nelson repeated, "It's northwest of here, about a ten-hour drive."

"Oh," Peta mouthed silently, not wanting to interrupt again, but her mind was reeling. Ten hours, and how long after she dropped him off would she be on the road before she arrived back in Rockhampton.

Nelson continued, "I've been given the task of trying to appease a local landowner who recently purchased a piece of equipment from us that appears to be faulty."

"But why can't you drive out there yourself, or better still, fly?" Peta wanted to know. She didn't know why she was bothering to argue the point with him, because he always won any verbal battle between the two of them.

"No reason. I'll probably fly home. Don't you want my company, Jupiter? You're always complaining that we don't see enough of each other anymore. Here's your chance to spend the day with me," he teased, throwing her one of his most winning smiles, before adding, "It will give us time to catch up. If we leave bright and early tomorrow morning, we can be in Tambo by late afternoon. There's a nice motel in town where we can spend the night. Then you can be on your way back to Rocky."

"You make it sound so simple. How much more driving do I have to do after dropping you off?" she had wanted to know.

"About another eight or nine hours."

"Wonderful." Peta was sorry she'd asked, for she already knew that she was going to accompany Nelson on this harebrained trip. It really didn't help to know that she had two full days of driving ahead of her.

A sharp tapping on her window quickly brought her back to the present, and to her current dilemma. Looking intently through the rain smeared pane of glass, it dismayed her to see a soaked, bedraggled man peering inquiringly in at her. He was making a winding motion with one of his hands, wanting her to wind down the window. Her moment of alarm must have been clear to him, for he stepped back from the car, allowing her to view him more clearly through the drizzle. Realising that this wasn't a situation where common sense could prevail, Peta gingerly wound down her window by the merest fraction, answering the man's silent plea. She wasn't in a position where she could simply turn the key in the ignition and drive off leaving her would be assailant behind, but if she was to be honest with herself he didn't look to be dangerous, only very wet and slightly annoyed at her reluctance to open her window to him.

Peta slowly inched the window down further, allowing only the smallest space to appear before asking him suspiciously, "What do you want?" She continued to eye him cautiously from the relevant safety of her car.

"A lift would be nice, possibly to the next service station." Rivulets of water were running down his face and into his eyes, which struck Peta as being the most vibrant shade of green she'd ever seen.

"Oh . . . ," she spluttered, nervously asking him, "Where is your car?" this man had literally crept up on her, scaring her out of her wits. Was she now supposed to open the door to him, to give him a lift? For all she knew, he could be a rapist, or even worse, a murderer.

He turned, showing with a quick flick of his head, to a spot further down the road, and as Peta's eyes followed his gaze she could just make out through the gathering darkness a vehicle resting on the verge of the highway.

"I'd really appreciate a lift unless you're too busy admiring the scenery, or are you just taking a short tea break?" he asked her. His voice held the merest hint of sarcasm.

"Neither," she shot back at him, taking her cue from his sarcastic comment, then added in a more subdued manner, "I have a puncture. I was thinking about getting out to fix it when you happened along."

"Really," the look he directed at her spoke volumes. It said here is another useless female who shouldn't be allowed out by herself, "Well, I'll make a deal with you. I'll fix your puncture if you give me a lift. That way we can help each other out. There's not much sense in our both getting soaked. What do you say?"

He had gone down onto his haunches and Peta could look straight into his eyes. He didn't flinch from her stare, but held her eyes with his own, letting Peta judge for herself if he was to be trusted. The rain had entirely drenched him and his clothes clung to his body like a second skin, showing her the muscled strength of his body. If she agreed to give him a lift and her instincts proved to be wrong, she knew she would be quickly overpowered. On the other hand, she knew that if she left him to suffer the fate of the elements that he'd be in for a long, miserable wait, with the possibility of not being able to get another lift for the rest of the night. In the half hour that she'd been sitting here by the side of the road there hadn't been a vehicle of any description pass her by in either direction, and although she wasn't in the habit of picking up hitch-hikers, she had to admit to herself that these were extenuating circumstances. Anyway, she reasoned, she needed his help as much as he needed hers. They would be helping each other out of a bind.

She informed him of her decision by saying simply, "The jack's in the boot." Reaching down beside her seat, she pulled a lever and the boot automatically swung upwards.

He didn't answer, giving her a curt nod instead as he made his way towards the rear of the car. Peta silently watched him and prayed that she would be safe; that her would be guardian angel wouldn't misinterpret her kind gesture and take advantage of her offered kindness. While he was changing the tyre, Peta covertly watched him through the side-view mirror. He looked like a man who made his living out of doors. His skin was deeply tanned, reminding Peta of a bronzed statue. She knew the highway bordered on cattle country, so perhaps he worked on one of the properties which were scattered throughout the district. He seemed competent and sure of himself as he deftly went about his task, giving Peta the impression that he definitely knew his way around a vehicle. It was only a matter of minutes before he was easing his agile frame in next to hers.

Peta's earlier bravado deserted her, and she was at a loss for words. She felt dwarfed and totally unsure of herself, not knowing what she should say or do next. Breaking the silence that was threatening to engulf them, she offered him a towel, which was on the back seat. He was completely saturated and must have felt uncomfortable sitting in his wet clothes.

Nodding his thanks, he removed his hat and Peta was instantly reminded of ravens wings. His hair was coal black, and even though it was dripping wet, she could see how thick and healthy the dark locks looked. He pushed the wet strands back from his face with long, lean fingers. "Not that it will do me much good, but thanks anyway. I'm sorry about getting everything wet, but I'm not in a position where I can change clothes."

He has a worker's hand, Peta thought as she gazed at him. She noticed his nails were clipped short and were immaculately clean, except for a few dark smudges of grease, probably from changing the tyre. His right hand had a jagged scar which started above his wrist and continued downwards towards his fingers. Peta stared intently when she realised that his little finger was missing. She wondered what kind of accident would cause someone to lose their finger.

She was appalled when he held his hand out towards her for a closer inspection, telling her casually, "I lost it many years ago when I was fencing with my father."

"I'm sorry. I didn't mean to stare." Peta could feel her face turning a violent crimson and was thankful for the growing darkness which was rapidly descending around them. She grabbed onto the first thing that came into her head, asking him if he'd like to get any belongings from his car before they headed off.

"Actually, yes, I would just in case I can't get the car fixed straight away. Then, at least, I can get into some dry clothes."

Casting him a nervous look, Peta was regretting her offer of a lift, but she couldn't very well have driven off, leaving him stranded after he'd stood in the pouring rain to fix her puncture. She reasoned that he'd made an innocent remark, for he was indeed sopping wet. He had probably just been trying to start the makings of a conversation. She wasn't one to engage in idle conversation for conversation's sake, but preferred to remain silent. She fervently hoped he wasn't waiting for her to answer him with a flirtatious innuendo, for if that was the case, he was going to be sadly disappointed. Although she had to grudgingly admit that he was drop dead gorgeous even in this bedraggled, wet state. Under any circumstances, she knew he was a man who would stand out in a crowd.

Peta was glad to be on the move because it meant she had to concentrate on her driving and not on the handsome stranger sitting in such close proximity next to her, but she found her mind continually wandered back to the man who sat quietly beside her. She wondered about his eventual destination, where he'd been going. Was he on his way home, or was he on his way to meet someone? He had other clothes with him, but that meant nothing. He could be on his way home just as surely as he could be going somewhere. She found she couldn't ask him any of the questions which cluttered her mind. Being a city girl, Peta couldn't say for sure if his clothes were fashionable, but she recognised quality when she saw it. He wore faded gabardine jeans which closely hugged his slim hips and manly thighs, and his shirt was a khaki colour, which he wore with the sleeves rolled up over his muscled forearms. If he was on his way into town to meet someone, a girl perhaps, Peta hoped his girlfriend was the understanding type, because she feared it would be many hours before he reached his final destination.

Although many questions raced through her mind about her passenger, she didn't voice any of them to him personally, feeling it was safer not to know anything about him. In her increased state of nervousness, Peta crunched the gears as she negotiated a sharp bend in the road. Biting the side of her lip, she was determined not to look at her passenger for fear he'd say something derisive about her driving skills, and women drivers in particular, but at the last minute she stole a quick glance in his direction and was appalled to see that he was indeed looking across at her. She couldn't read his expression in the growing darkness, but she was sure he threw her a look of pure incompetence.

"My foot slipped," she lied to protect herself from the quip, which she was sure was going to follow that enquiring stare. But he said nothing, settling back once more into the comfort of his seat. When she realised he wasn't going to engage in worthless conversation, she relaxed and began to appreciate the countryside through which they were passing. They had left the rain behind, but dark clouds still obliterated most of the sky. Dusk had fallen, and the shadows had nearly disappeared, giving way to night. She could just make out a large flock of cockatoos as they made their way homewards to roost for the night. She imagined the noise they'd be making, calling to each other as they finally settled into the many trees which could be seen dotting the paddocks along the edge of the highway.

It brought home to her how isolated and vulnerable she felt sitting next to this stranger and she wondered if she should try to start up a conversation with him after all, but found that she was unable to form the words needed in order for her to do so. She was nervous and just a little scared of the situation she found herself in.

A lengthy silence had passed between them when a slight movement at her side brought her instantly out of her reverie, and her mind was drawn back to the person sitting beside her. She couldn't stop the slight tremor which coursed throughout her body as she chanced a slight glance in his direction. He appeared to be asleep, his large frame taking up every available bit of space on his side of the car.

Without really knowing why, Peta studied him in the darkness, which provided a perfect screen for her scrutiny of him. The lights from the dashboard of her car threw out sufficient light so that she could make out his relaxed features. Her opinion about his good looks hadn't altered. She still thought his profile was very pleasing. He makes great eye candy, but she wasn't foolish enough to think that good looks alone automatically meant that a person had a good heart.

Peta wondered idly what her companion's name was. She supposed she should have introduced herself before they started out on this ridiculous journey, but at the time introductions hadn't been high on her agenda of things to do. She'd been afraid, and her fears had cut off any of the pleasantries that might have passed between them on this trip.

Her mind registered the fact that he was very tall, probably well over six feet, if Peta was any judge. He was well built and his body, even in rest, belied a hidden strength which she was sure he could call upon and harness. Dark whiskers had started to show along his strong jawline, and before long he'd need to shave. He wore boots. They looked like they were made of excellent quality leather. Probably J. M. Williams, she thought absently. When she put these facts together Peta concluded he might not be the lowly station hand she had taken him to be during her earlier evaluation of his character.

Her attention was momentarily drawn back to the road, as she had to negotiate some winding curves which required her full concentration because of the heavy rain which had, again, started to fall. Almost immediately, the rain stopped and Peta was able to relax her tight grip on the steering wheel. She had never enjoyed driving in the rain, and never would.

The world outside the car was completely dark now, and Peta wasn't able to make out any of the countryside through which they were driving. With every bend in the road, she looked expectantly for a service station where she could drop him off with a good conscience. Finally, her search was brought to an abrupt end when she saw bright glowing lights in the distance which signalled that they were approaching a service station. She'd be able to drop him off and be on her way. She wondered foolishly if she should introduce herself before she said goodbye, but then she dismissed the idea as being silly. He'd think she was a fool. Now that their forced journey was ending, Peta wished they had at least exchanged names. She would have to thank him for fixing the puncture, if nothing else.

Peta felt him stirring in the seat next to her and looked across to see him watching her. "We're here, but I don't know exactly where here is," she told him unnecessarily as she guided the car up to a vacant petrol bowser. She felt the knots in her stomach tightening as she returned his stare.

"So I see," he told her casually as he took in his surroundings.

"You shouldn't have any trouble getting your car towed in from here. At least it looks like they have a mechanic on duty," she said, showing with a toss of her head towards the large mechanic's bay where even now she could see work being carried out on several cars. Peta knew she was babbling, but she couldn't seem to help herself. She needed to let him know that this was where he got out.

"Probably not," he drawled in a voice that was deep and vibrant. In other circumstances, she knew she would have found listening to him a very pleasing experience.

"Um . . . thank you for fixing my puncture. I'd probably still be sitting on the side of the road if you hadn't happened along." Peta could hear the wobble in her voice and prayed that he wouldn't guess the reason behind her discomfort. She purposely opened her door and stepped out, leaving him with no option but to do the same.

"You're welcome. Thank you for the lift." His voice had a mocking quality to it, and Peta eyed him suspiciously. They sounded like two people swapping pleasantries for the lack of nothing better to do.

"Well, I'm going to get some petrol and something to eat before I leave so . . . um . . . good luck with your car." She walked backwards away from him, wondering if she should say anything else, but her mind had emptied, turning into a blank vacuum which she couldn't penetrate. She could think of nothing to add, so saying another hurried farewell, she turned and fled towards the ladies' room, where she heaved a huge sigh of relief.

Taking the time to wash her face and comb her hair, Peta critically studied her reflection under the harsh fluorescent lights of the restroom. Dark circles encircled her eyes, and Peta didn't need the mirror to tell her just how tired she was feeling. The face that looked back at her was pale and wan, a sure sign that she needed a good night's sleep. Her hair, usually a vibrant, healthy brown, hung lacklustre and dank around her shoulders. She was quick to concede that she was definitely not looking her best, having opted not to wear make-up, as she hadn't thought it necessary to fix herself up for the long drive back to Rockhampton. Even her clothes were crumpled. She had chosen a favourite faded purple T-shirt that had seen better days and her shorts had been chosen because they were comfortable, but she told herself consolingly as she looked at her image in the mirror, "At least your figure still looks okay," but these words brought her little consolation as she thought of the man she had just left, "No wonder he didn't show any interest in you. You look terrible."

Peta had viewed herself with a slightly biased eye, for on more than one occasion in the past her attractive looks and soft feminine curves had attracted appreciative looks from members of the opposite sex.

Venturing outside a short time later, Peta scanned her surroundings, looking for his familiar face, but he was nowhere to be seen. She was glad to be rid of him, although he hadn't posed a threat to her person. She was forced to smile as she recalled the picture of herself she had just seen in the restroom. No wonder he didn't pay any attention to her. He probably thinks I'm not attractive enough to bother about.

She found her mind was dredging up the last hour spent in the close confines of her car with him, and her body trembled from the suppressed emotion she had been feeling. In this day and age, a person had to be extremely careful who they associated with. She could have been sharing her car with a maniac. One just didn't know.

"Anyway, it's all water under the bridge now," she told herself. "He's gone and I'll never see him again." She was reminded of ships that pass in the night, passing so close to each other, but never getting close enough to really see what the other vessel looked like.

Grabbing a quick bite to eat, Peta was eager to be on her way. She had been informed that she still had at least three hours of driving ahead of her before she reached her final destination. She glanced around the room as she sat eating her meal. Her stomach lurched painfully when she spied him through the plate-glass window. He was talking to someone whom she presumed to be the mechanic, for the young man was dressed in overalls. They were covered with a healthy smattering of grease. Peta found her eyes were drawn to her travelling companion. She took in his casual stance, but even so, she was quick to recognise the authority which seemed to emanate from him. This man was used to issuing orders, not receiving them, of that she was now certain. She thought he'd be long gone by now and hoped that fate wouldn't let him look in her direction.

He was openly laughing at something that had been said to him, and Peta, from her hidden position behind the glass windows, was treated to a burst of pure sunshine. His body language spoke volumes, and Peta was getting the message loud and clear. She found she'd been correct about his height. He was extremely tall and well-muscled. His shirt, although nearly dry, still clung to his chest and back, revealing a body which was obviously used to hard work. He was holding his hat in one hand, while his free hand was hooked casually into the top pocket of his jeans.

He and the mechanic were joined by a third person, another man, and Peta watched them unashamedly. He was listening to something they were saying and suddenly he grinned, nodding his head in obvious agreement. Peta thought it was a pleasant smile and found herself wishing she could have been the recipient of a similar gesture while they'd been together.

Heavens, from where in her mind did that notion manifest itself, Peta thought, as she continued to stare blatantly at him. There was a deep abyss in her mind into which she refused to delve. Perhaps she had lodged her initial memory of him there, and it was now coming to the surface to haunt her. But he hadn't smiled at her; he hadn't approached her except to ask for a lift. She thought if circumstances had been different, she would have found him very appealing, perhaps even to the extent of wanting to further their relationship, to nourish it and let it flourish into something vibrant and real. But, of course, for something like that to take place, there had to be a stable foundation to build upon, and that was something they would never have. They didn't have a relationship of any kind, nor were they ever likely to. Their time together was well and truly past. In fact, Peta had to remind herself it had never been. To him, she had been a means to an end, someone who had given him a lift, and grudgingly at that, from point A to point B.

Peta felt a pang of something akin to remorse pass through her, telling herself she had missed a wonderful opportunity to experience something grand in her life. I must really be tired to be wallowing in so much self-pity, Peta thought to herself. Anyway, she added, who's to say that he would've felt the same way. Perhaps I'm not his type. Perhaps that's why he was content to remain silent. Maybe he has a girlfriend, or maybe he's married . . .

Waiting until he had moved off with the mechanic towards the waiting tow truck, Peta thought it was safe to make her escape and she finally made a move toward her car. She thought she would be safe, that he would be gone, but as soon as she walked out through the large sliding glass doors the tow truck rolled into view, stopping just a few metres in front of her, literally blocking her way. The driver stepped out of the cab, telling his passenger he wouldn't be long.

She didn't have to look into the dark confines of the cab to guess who the sole occupant was. Fate seemed to be playing cruel tricks, putting him constantly in her path. It would be rude of her to walk past and not acknowledge his presence, but if she did speak to him, what was she expected to say? There were just so many pleasantries that two people could exchange with each other in one day, and Peta thought ruefully that she had definitely used up her quota. This situation was getting comical from Peta's point of view and she suppressed a slight smile by covering her mouth with her hand, pretending to blow her nose with a tissue. She found it ironic that they hadn't conversed at all while they were travelling in her car, but now that he was about to drive away in the mechanic's company, she felt the need to speak to him just because they'd had the misfortune to cross paths yet again.

She was saved from uttering a single word, for just as she was gathering her courage to walk across to him to ask if he was finally on his way to get his car the mechanic came out of the large double doors behind her and walked purposely towards the truck where he leaned his large frame on the window sill thus blocking her view of the man sitting inside.

Peta hurried past, thankful that she had been spared the ordeal of talking to him, although she had to admit to herself that she now felt slightly cheated out of her last chance to communicate with him.

What a load of rot, she told herself. You can't have it both ways. Either he's someone you want to see again or he isn't. Anyway, she reasoned, the choice was never yours to make. You will never see him again. This thought saddened her because for some inexplicable reason Peta was drawn to this man.

Upon reaching her car, she was surprised to see a small, neat package had been strategically wedged underneath one of the car's windscreen wipers. Picking up the parcel with trembling fingers, Peta pondered what she should do next. She could feel a knot forming in the pit of her stomach as she opened the package wondering what in the world a virtual stranger would find to give her as a way of saying thank you for there wasn't a single doubt in her mind that the package was from her handsome stranger.

On opening the dainty package, it surprised her to see a delicate gold necklace with a small gold cross which was embedded with a small blue stone. The necklace lay enfolded in a silky bed of blue satin which helped to emphasise its lovely golden colour. There was an inscription printed on the lid of the box, and Peta felt sure it was these words that had drawn his attention to the gift. She read, "The wearer of this cross will always be protected from all worldly things, for she will have the might of God to protect her and to be with her always."

Peta didn't doubt that he was mocking her in some small way by giving her this gift. He was telling her he hadn't been a threat to her safety; she was sure of it, but now it was too late to do anything about it for the truck was pulling out onto the highway, its occupants were engaged in conversation, but just as the vehicle was about to speed away he looked over towards Peta, giving her a small silent salute as a final gesture of farewell. Subconsciously, Peta raised her hand, waving goodbye as she watched him disappear into the night.

Thinking about their short time together, Peta found she was regretting her silence. She'd been scared of him. He'd been an unknown factor and just because he'd turned out to be halfway decent didn't mean that she had to stop to pick up every stranded traveller she happened across in the course of her travels in the future. No, she'd been very lucky, that was all. She must always remember that.

Life was so unpredictable, she thought to herself. One minute you're fancy free with the world at your feet with no cares or worries to speak of and then in less than a heartbeat your entire way of thinking can be changed by a set of circumstances over which you have not a scrap of control. Peta thought about her paternal grandmother and the major role this strong-minded woman had played in her life, how her passing had changed Peta's lifestyle and consequently her general outlook on the world at large.

She pondered yet again how happiness could directly result from grief and sadness. Why had her beloved Nan had to die? She had been Peta's last living relative. In the end, age had been her greatest adversary. They had celebrated Nan's ninety-fourth birthday just a few months before she died. Peta smiled fondly as she remembered her grandparent. She had never allowed her age to slow her down or to be a deterrent to anything that she had set out to do. She had remained quick witted and extremely agile until the very end, when the Lord had taken her peacefully in her sleep.

Peta had been the sole beneficiary of her grandmother's estate, being her only living relative. It had surprised her to learn from the family solicitor that she was to inherit a tidy sum of money and the house that had been her home for the last ten years. The money had been skilfully invested for her over several years.

Peta had always fostered a dream, one which she often shared with her grandmother. She wanted to open an arts and craft shop, not a dream of earth shattering importance by any stretch of the imagination, but a dream none the less. Nan had always smiled, telling her to follow her dream, to reach out with both hands grabbing onto her vision.

After Nan's funeral, Peta had been presented with a letter from their solicitor, who told her he had been instructed to personally place the letter into her hands and to help her with any subsequent arrangements which might have to be carried out. Mr. Doubel had been a tower of strength and Peta had learnt to count on him totally for legal advice. Together, they had scoured the local papers looking for a suitable property where Peta could establish her arts and craft shop.

Finally, an excellent location had presented itself, but to Peta's dismay it would mean moving to Rockhampton, further up the Queensland coast. Still, she was overjoyed at the prospect of realising her dream. There had been the added bonus of an adjoining apartment at the back of the building. It was tiny, but it would meet all of Peta's needs perfectly. There was even room to store surplus stock. Peta had planned to move in as soon as she was able. Fifteen months had passed since she first opened her doors to the public.

The house she'd shared with her grandmother had been sold. By doing this, Peta was creating a cash flow which would help her in the initial stages of her business. Stock had to be purchased, and the premises had to be fitted out. Peta had decided right from the start that she was going to create a welcoming atmosphere which customers would find appealing, thus not feeling the need to rush away, and hopefully, making them feel as if they would want to come back.

In one corner, Peta had set up a small couch and a table upon which there was always an urn on the boil should anyone feel like a hot drink of tea or coffee. With this one small gesture, she was making it perfectly clear that it was alright to come in and chat for a while. She was also toying with the idea of starting up a kids' corner so that the mums could browse at their leisure, safely knowing that their precious offspring were safely tucked away out of harm's way. She smiled as she remembered how she had on one occasion offered one young mother the use of her bathroom when her little girl had had an accident. The woman had been extremely grateful for Peta's kindness and was now a regular customer and a friend.

This was the third buying trip which Peta had made in the last twelve months. Sometimes she liked to purchase her stock in person. She didn't want to take the chance of purchasing goods, which didn't meet with her approval. It also gave her the chance to meet with the people she hoped to do business with over the course of the coming years. She wanted to establish a good working relationship with the companies, and subsequently, with the personnel involved. Peta had opted to keep her prices down as much as possible, liking to pass some savings on to her customers. She was making a healthy profit with more than enough left over to purchase new stock regularly. It gave her a sense of well-being when a customer remarked about her prices. She knew she was selling her products at a slightly cheaper rate than any of her competitors, but she believed it was her friendliness and willingness to help which brought people back into her shop.

Lately, she'd been toying with the idea of starting a mail order service for people who weren't able to avail themselves of her products directly. The more she thought about this idea, the more it appealed to her. There were plenty of people living in remote areas who would jump at the chance of having an opportunity such as this. Peta knew services like the one she wanted to introduce already existed, but as far as she knew, only the large department stores had taken up the challenge. It would mean a lot of extra work if the idea took off, establishing a client list and producing a working catalogue, but Peta thought it would be worth the effort. Her shop could cater to customers wanting the specialised items that could only be found in an arts and craft shop such as hers.

She planned to stock a bit of everything eventually, but that would mean expanding the premises and that, she knew, would have to be a few more years down the track. She could see the positive side of branching out into other areas of the art world. Already, she carried a large range of merchandise for the local porcelain doll makers, having arranged with one supplier on the Sunshine Coast a few months earlier. This had proved to be a successful gamble. As a doll maker herself, she knew how long it could take to get the bits and pieces which were required to finish a doll.

On this trip, she had purchased a kiln, which was to be delivered at a later date. She hoped she would find the time to pursue her fervent passion for pottery, ceramics and porcelain doll making. Since starting her own business, she'd had to shelve several personal projects on which she had worked, but she had promised herself she was going to make some time for her own projects in the future. Since moving north, Peta found she didn't spend as much time socialising as she probably should. Her shop took up most of her days and nights, which meant she spent a lot of her free time with only herself for company. When she did venture out, she went by herself and then it was usually to the movies, or to a gallery showing, and sometimes she treated herself to a play whenever there was a musical in production at the Pilbeam Theatre. She had a passion for musicals. She was content with her life and couldn't think of any reason she would want to change the way she lived.

All in all, she was satisfied with her life, so why, now, was she sitting here, in her car, in the middle of nowhere, analysing her life in such minute detail? Why should a chance encounter with this particular man trip off such feelings within her? She didn't think she was missing out by not having a man to escort her to the places she visited. She wasn't mourning the loss of a man in her life.

Peta idly fingered the fine gold chain in her hand, thinking once more of the man who had given this gift to her.

The next few days were extremely busy ones for Peta. After working long hours in the shop all day, she filled the shelves with the new stock which had arrived the day before. She wished, not for the first time, that her grandmother was here to share her happiness. Her business was thriving, and she was adding new lines of stock regularly to her already well-stocked shelves. She desperately missed her grandmother and the talks they used to have on anything and everything. No subject had been taboo between them.

Her customers were becoming regulars, but more than this, they were becoming friends with Peta and with each other. Peta's friendliness and good-hearted nature drew them like flies to a honey pot. On more than one occasion, she had been inundated with people who were happy to stay and work on their individual projects here in the shop. They would set themselves up in an available corner where they would talk over a cup of hot brew about their respective families and generally have a friendly laugh and share friendship and fellowship for an hour or so.

She had received a phone call earlier in the day from Nelson. He had told her he'd be passing through Rockhampton on business early in the week and would leave sometime Saturday. He arranged a night for them to have dinner together, telling her that if he had the time he would treat her to the movies as long as he could choose the flick they saw. She smiled to herself. Nelson had been adamant about this one issue. He usually hated the movies she dragged him along to and would complain for the whole two hours about the movie that was on the screen.

Actually, it would be good to see Nelson again. She had long since forgiven him for the puncture that had left her stranded by the side of the highway.

"So tell me," Peta was saying as she served Nelson his meal, "What have you been up to lately? I'm completely out of touch with just about every single person I know."

"So I've been told." Nelson took a bite of the delicious smelling meal which had been placed before him and rolled his eyes heavenward as he chewed the tender morsels of meat "Koombyar, Jupiter, koombyar." It was something that he did and had always done since the very first time Peta had cooked for him when they'd been in home economics class way back in high school. It had become a sort of tradition, and Peta would have missed these words if they weren't forthcoming.

She had enjoyed preparing the meal for him. She didn't do a lot of cooking these days, mostly opting for a sandwich or some salad vegetables thrown haphazardly onto a plate.

"Getting back to the question of your friends, Jupiter, I have been asked, or delegated, depending on how you want to look at it, to give you several personal messages, each one is about your apparent lack of communication with your so-called friends. They all think you've given up on them and given them the old heave ho."

"Oh dear," Peta exclaimed, feeling a momentary stab of guilt as she thought of the trip she had recently returned from. There hadn't been a minute to spare to visit any of her friends this time, but she promised herself sincerely that she would make extra time to visit every one of them on her next trip south which would be in another couple of months to purchase yet more stock, "But that's not true. I've just been so incredibly busy trying to get the shop up and running over this past year. I guess I have been a bit lax, though. I'll definitely get in touch as soon as I can."

"Fine, just see that you do. You have many people who have been worrying about your welfare," he told her bluntly, but truthfully. Jupiter had been well liked and respected, and it vexed him to see her cut herself off from the people who loved her. Seeing her look of consternation, he tacked on, "They understand, Jupiter."

To keep from becoming upset by the line their conversation was taking, she latched on to the first coherent thought to enter her mind. Anything was preferable to thinking about the past and the mistake she had come so very close to making. "Why must you persist in calling me Jupiter? You know I like to be called Peta. Why my parents picked a name like that, I'll never know. They obviously knew nothing about my namesake." Nelson had heard it all before, so she didn't go into the spiel about the planet like she normally would to a complete stranger. Complete stranger! Her mind wandered briefly back to the tall, handsome man she had given a lift to. She wondered where he was. What was he doing? Did he get his car fixed?

Nelson was saying, "Earth to Jupiter, come in, over."

Peta stared at him blankly before realising he was trying to reclaim her attention. When he saw she was listening to him again, he continued, "That's better. Now where was I, oh yes, I remember. I was telling you I would rather call you Jupiter because I like the name Jupiter. It suits you and you know how I hate to shorten names. Call it a fetish if you like."

Peta sighed audibly as she looked across at her friend. She knew better than to argue with him because she always lost her verbal battles with this man. "Fine, you win. Now what movie do you want to see?" She asked pleasantly, already knowing which film she intended dragging him along to.

"None, I'm afraid," he answered before adding dolefully as he watched the play of emotion wash across Peta's face, changing her features from expectant anticipation to complete disappointment in the space of a

The Grazier's Proposal

few quick seconds. "Don't look like that. I had to squeeze this time with you out of a very hectic schedule, as it was. I have meetings for the whole of the time that I'm here, so I'm afraid you'll have to go solo, my sweet girl."

"Must I," Peta's disappointment was genuine for she had really been looking forward to this time spent with her friend.

"Afraid so," Nelson told her as he rose to his feet. "I have to meet someone in less than half an hour. This is, after all, a business trip, Jupiter, but there's no reason you can't go by yourself, is there? It won't be the first time you've gone out by yourself. As I remember, you were never one to mind going out by yourself. Don't tell me you're going soft in your old age."

"I know all that, but I was looking forward to your company. When am I going to see you again?" Peta asked him, already missing her friend.

"I'm not sure when I'll be up this way again. It will depend on the powers that be, but I promise that I'll make sure I clear a specific amount of time from my calendar so that we'll be able to do whatever your heart desires." He was reaching for his car keys as he spoke, which showed Peta that time was indeed a valuable commodity to him at the moment.

She gave him an obedient kiss on the cheek and then forlornly waved him goodbye until his car had turned the corner and was out of sight. The thought of going to a movie alone didn't especially appeal to Peta, but she needed to get out, to be among other people, even if it was in a darkened cinema where every person was a complete stranger. She had been possessed with a restlessness lately, one which she didn't fully understand, and it baffled her not being able to pinpoint the cause of her dissatisfaction within her own life. She was probably working too hard. Giving long hours to the running of the shop satisfied the artistic side of her persona, but what about the other part of her life, the personal side, which was slowly starving to death because of a lack of adequate nutrition? Male company, her mind prompted casually. A bit of male company wouldn't go astray now and again, you know. That's ridiculous, she told herself resolutely; I don't need the company of a man to make me happy.

Peta had had a friend in Brisbane. Cody, they'd hung out together, accompanying each other to the various parties they'd get invited to. At one time, Peta had hoped that it might go further, but it hadn't. She was okay with it, so why think about it now?

No, she wasn't going to reconstruct old memories. The past was dead and buried and couldn't be resurrected. It was over, and it was better to leave it that way. She had made the choice to move to Rockhampton, to move after the death of her grandmother, so she wouldn't regret the fact that she didn't have any friends to speak of outside the shop. Her acquaintances from the shop all had husbands and families who demanded their attention, especially now during the non-daylight hours when they were home. Peta knew that eventually she'd build up a circle of friends, but she thought unhappily to herself, they wouldn't take the place of the people she had left behind. She had asked Cody to come with her, but he had refused her offer to move to Rockhampton, not wanting to leave the close knit community of which they had been a part.

Chapter Two

ONCE AT THE CINEMA Peta found she had a wide variety of movies to choose from and because of her flagging spirits she prescribed a comedy for herself, hoping that a laugh would help ease her low mood and restore her happy composure.

Settling herself into her seat, noting appreciatively that they were extremely comfortable, she munched on her popcorn, which she saw as a perfect accompaniment to any movie. Having kicked off her sandals, her bare feet were now resting lightly on the back of the seat in front of her. Peta believed in being comfortable if she was to sit for two hours in a darkened room. She had chosen an area of the cinema that had been less populated, not liking to be squashed in, or to have people in front of her who liked to fidget in their seats throughout the whole of the movie.

Patrons were still trickling in to take their seats, and Peta looked at them with a semi-detached interest, wondering about the people who shared her interest in this movie genre. Her attention was arrested moments later as she saw one particular couple heading up the aisle towards her.

Oh no! It was that man! Her companion! No, not her companion. He hadn't been that! To call him a companion would mean that they'd shared each other's company when all they had shared was space.

Her hand flew involuntarily to the small cross which was hanging around her neck. Vivid memories of him, and their short time together came flooding back to haunt her, and she found herself, yet again, wishing that she had started up some sort of conversation with him because if that had been the case she wouldn't be feeling so desperate and awkward now. She could smile up at him in a friendly manner to ask how he was going and so forth, to pass the time of day, if only for a minute before he passed her by.

She looked away in terror, afraid that he'd notice her, but a small part of her was also afraid that he'd pass her by without giving her a second glance. Anyway, she told herself, he probably doesn't remember me. They had only been in each other's company for a little over an hour, not enough time to make a lasting impression on anyone. Still, as he and his companion moved up the aisle, coming ever closer to her, her heart pounded chaotically, and she found she was having difficulty in catching her breath. She threw some popcorn into her mouth, thinking that if she had something to do, she might regain some semblance of her crumbling self-control.

To her horror, she coughed as the popcorn lodged itself firmly in her throat. Her timing for disaster was still spot on. He was almost beside her; Peta could see the perfect shine of his shoes, even in the semi-darkness of the theatre. She tried to regulate her breathing, trying to stop the fit of coughing, which was causing heads in the theatre to turn inquisitively in her direction. Her eyes had filled with watery tears because of her incessant bout of coughing. She almost wished she would choke. At least then she would be out of her misery, and this embarrassing episode would be at an end.

"Lean forward!" came a familiar voice from somewhere above her. It was laced with authority and sounded like it wasn't going to brook any argument.

Peta, unable to respond verbally, did as she'd been commanded to do. She could feel a vivid heat rising from her neck to cover her cheeks and was thankful for the darkness which now engulfed her.

A firm hand slapped her on the back several times, thus dislodging the piece of confectionery, putting an end to her bout of coughing.

Totally embarrassed, she looked up at him, wiping the flow of tears from her eyes as she did so. She must look a sight, but a thank you of some kind had to be offered. Perhaps he was just helping a person in need, but as Peta looked up into his face, she could see by his stare that he recognised her. Another blush tinged her face as he looked down at her from what seemed to be a very great height from where she sat slouched in her chair. She wished she could get up and walk out, but that wouldn't serve any purpose, which she could logically think of.

"Thank you," she mumbled, unsure of what she should say next. What exactly did one say to someone who had dragged you back from death's door? Peta knew she was being melodramatic, but her emotions had been heightened by the entire experience of the last few minutes?

"You're welcome. I'm sure you'll live. Enjoy the movie," he told her, walking off as his companion implored him impatiently to sit down before the movie started.

Peta was acutely aware of his presence throughout the whole of the film, and her concentration was totally shattered. She couldn't interest herself in the plot, or the characters. Her mind was constantly being drawn to that man and his companion. She had never known two hours to drag so slowly, feeling as if she had lived an entire lifetime during the film.

The fact that he was sitting just a few rows behind her was unnerving. Was he watching her? Or had he forgotten about her existence as soon as he had moved away? She knew with a heartfelt certainty that it would be the latter. How could he have thoughts of her when he was accompanied by such a gorgeous creature as the woman who now sat next to him as his companion?

Peta's mind fostered images of herself as she compared herself to the other woman's flawless beauty. She recalled long golden tresses which waved freely down the other woman's back in a thick mass reaching almost to her neat, trim waist. She had been well dressed and immaculately made up, making Peta wish she had taken more time with her own tawdry appearance. The woman had been tall, and Peta had to admit, although reluctantly, that they made a striking couple, one that would certainly turn heads wherever they went. He with his raven black locks interwoven with the lovely blond strands of his companion.

Peta wondered if they were married. If they weren't married, it would only be a matter of time before the blonde woman would march him down the aisle, Peta concluded. She found this thought disturbed her more than she cared to admit, but she wouldn't let herself speculate on any other details. For instance, why should his marriage or impending marriage to this woman upset her; If he was already a candidate in the marriage stakes, it was hardly any of her business.

In his line of work it would be extremely dangerous to wear a wedding band, she thought absently. She remembered his missing finger and was overcome by an overwhelming urge to kiss the joint where the digit had been so forcibly removed in the first place when he had only been a small child. She had shocked herself by this line of thinking and therefore quickly pushed the errant thought back into the hidden recesses of her mind, where such blatant thoughts couldn't manifest themselves into her consciousness. It was safer to delegate such a thought to the back of her mind, or she would be in danger of losing her sanity.

As soon as the finishing credits appeared on the screen, Peta literally bolted out of her seat, heading for the exit. She didn't want to risk bumping into him again. She wouldn't know how to act or how to respond to any attempt at conversation which he might try to initiate.

It occurred to her that if he was still here in town, he may not be a man who worked on the land as she had at first suspected. Seeing him also answered another question she had asked herself about his eventual destination being

Queensland's beef capital, but judging by his companion, cattle weren't the only draw card in the region.

Although he might come in from time to time to see his friend, she couldn't imagine he would want to spend long periods of time apart from the woman he was involved with. Peta had heard of couples spending their married life apart because the wife couldn't stand the loneliness of station life, thus making it necessary for the husband to travel great distances to see the love of his life. Somehow she couldn't envisage this man agreeing to conditions such as that. He would want a hands on marriage, nothing less would do for this man of the open plains.

Peta's shop had one small recurring problem which caused her an enormous amount of irritation. Every so often, the power would cut out, plunging the premises into an eerie gloominess until she could trip the switch in the cable box attached to the back of the building, which would again turn the lights back on.

Peta had been assured that this was a minor problem, which would be immediately fixed. It was disconcerting to have the lights go out when she was with a potential customer. She was afraid that this slight glitch in the running of things would turn customers away. Actually, she'd been giving a lot of thought to rent new premises and had started to look in the paper, wanting to know how she'd fare financially if she was to consider this proposal seriously because it would mean finding somewhere else to live. She doubted if she would be lucky enough to find another shop, which offered adjoining living quarters as well. Perhaps she should mention it to the Realtor next time she paid her rent. She knew it was tantamount to a threat, but something had to be done about the faulty wiring in the building.

Peta had been having a harrowing day. The power had gone out three times in the space of an hour. She was getting extremely irritated at having to put up with what she now saw as a major inconvenience. Last night after she had closed the doors of the shop she had phoned several electricians hoping one would come to her rescue, but she had been curtly informed that they didn't do after-hours calls unless she was willing to pay an exorbitant call out fee on top of their usual hourly rate to cover the cost of their being pulled out of a nice warm bed. She had told them all that they were highway robbers, adding hotly that if they had a shred of decency in their souls, they would forego an hour of their time to help someone in need without wanting to charge an arm and a leg before she slammed the phone down in their ear.

The age of chivalry is indeed dead, she thought to herself as she trudged outside once more to angrily flip the switch. No one wanted to help any more, just for the sake of helping. To lend a hand when it was needed was a dying art, and there didn't seem to be too many people interested in giving resuscitation.

The shop had been empty when she had trudged resignedly out the back to flip the switch and she was seriously thinking of closing the doors, hopping in her car and driving to the beach where she could let the sea breezes blow over her thus cooling her frayed temper and jangled nerves, but when she walked back into the now brightened room, a familiar face met her astonished eyes causing her to stop dead in her tracks.

It was him. How had he found her? What did he want? Was he here with anyone? Peta's eyes scanned the confines of her shop, looking for the blonde woman who had been his companion at the movies, but apart from the two of them, the shop was empty.

Peta congratulated herself on how well she could mask her surprise as she steadily made her way over to him. "Hello . . . did you want something?" she asked him politely before tacking on nervously, "or did you come here to see me?"

She knew this last question to be preposterous because how could he know where she worked, or even what her name was. How could he know! Surely he wasn't the kind of man who stalked women. She would have vowed with every instinct she possessed that this wasn't the case. No, this had to be another chance encounter between them. It was strange how they were always being thrown together, being placed into each other's company.

She thought she detected a momentary start of surprise as he returned her stare, but if so, it was quickly veiled.

"Hello," he answered casually in a voice that was becoming very familiar to her. "We seem to have developed a habit of running into each other." His voice had a deep, resonant quality that Peta found appealing. He had a slight drawl which gave his words a peaceful sound, but Peta was under no illusions because he was himself a man of action.

"Yes, it appears so. So, if you didn't come here specifically to see me you must be here to purchase something, or to at least look around." Peta thought he looked out of place amongst her ribbons and laces, but she kept this thought to herself. She wondered if she should strike up a conversation with him, asking him about his car. She would like to know how he'd fared.

"I've been given a list of supplies, so I think I'll just hand it over to the expert. I'm afraid I'm out of my element in these surroundings." Upon delivering these words, he fished a folded piece of paper out of his shirt pocket and handed it across to her. A slight smile covered his lips and this time Peta could actually detect a sparkling light present in his eyes, which reminded her of sunshine dancing on a lake at sunset.

"I wouldn't be game to go home without these things. I'd be skinned alive and left out for the ants to eat," he told her solemnly.

Peta smiled. She couldn't see anyone getting the better of him, but she kept her own counsel on these thoughts. After scanning the contents of the list, Peta was able to assure him she could supply most of the items on the rather long list.

"As for the rest," she told him lightly, "I'm sure you'll be able to pick them up around town." She smiled impishly as she pictured him venturing into the other establishments and felt her heart go out to him despite herself, responding to the slight frown which had settled onto his face.

"Look," she told him, wanting to help him out of his current dilemma, "why don't I get these other things for you? Can you call back later on this afternoon to pick them up?" The words were out of her mouth before she realised she had even uttered them.

"That would be nice. I'd really appreciate your help. I don't relish the thought of entering another female domain and having to ask for this stuff. The next proprietor might not be as helpful as you are," he told her, and Peta could hear the relief which was clearly evident in his voice. He continued, "If you're busy, you can do it all later on in the week. I'm here until Sunday, so there's no real hurry. I can come back Saturday afternoon and pick everything up then."

"Fine," Peta told him, "perhaps that would be better."

"Right. Until Saturday then," he tipped his hat before turning on his heel and was soon through the door and making his way across the street.

Peta was mesmerised by the sight of him, watching openly as his lengthy strides took him further away from her. Her gaze was shifted from him as some new customers made their way into the shop and when she looked in his direction again, he had disappeared from sight.

Saturday rolled around slowly and Peta glanced at the clock every few minutes, wondering why he hadn't turned up for his package. She was due to close the shop in ten minutes, but if he hadn't arrived by then she'd have no other choice but to remain open. She reluctantly admitted to herself that she hadn't told him when she finished work, so she couldn't entirely hold him to blame for not turning up on time.

"I'll make myself a cup of tea," she said to herself, "and then I'll do some quilting while I wait." This decision made, Peta settled down to wait for her mystery man as she now thought of him. She still didn't know his name, but she could instantly conjure up a perfect image of him into her mind. Doing so now brought a small smile of satisfaction to her lips, and she mentally chastised herself for her wayward thoughts. The absence of a wedding ring obviously didn't mean that he was free. Who else would he be buying laces and ribbons for? You can forget about the likes of him, Peta told herself sadly. He's way out of your reach.

Before too long, Peta was fully engrossed in the bedspread she had started to make for herself. She had admired a similar quilt in a movie she'd seen and had promised herself she would make one for herself. It wasn't an exact replica of the original, but Peta could see some similarities showing through in the design she had chosen.

Gathering up her empty teacup, she was just about to walk through to the back when the bell tingled loudly over the door. She had to hide the smile which instantly formed around the ridges of her mobile mouth when she recognised her customer as her mystery man.

"Hello," he said easily as his tall frame filled the doorway. "It seems I'm late." He was looking at the sign where the shop hours were displayed, before telling her contritely, "I'm sorry."

"That's okay," Peta told him truthfully. "It gave me a chance to work on some needlework. I've been able to get everything you wanted." She pulled a large parcel out from under the counter and slid it across to him.

"Fine," was his only comment as he pulled his wallet out of his hip pocket and paid for the goods.

Peta focused her gaze on his hands as she handed him his change, noticing again his long, lean fingers with their well-shaped nails. The forefinger on his left hand had a very large bruise under the nail, and Peta wondered how he'd gained such a wound. She had convinced herself that he did indeed work on the land, so probably the bruise resulted from a work-related incident.

He looked as if he was going to say something else as Peta looked up at him expectantly, but no words were forthcoming. She was saved from an awkward moment, wondering just what she should say to him, when her telephone rang.

Excusing herself, she answered the call, which brought an instant smile to her lips as she recognised the voice on the other end of the line.

Her eyes sparkled at this unexpected contact with her friend. "I thought you were well and truly on your way home," she told Nelson pertly and laughed delightedly into the mouthpiece when he informed her he was on his way over. He'd have a quick bite to eat with her, sharing a meal of fish and chips which he was supplying, he was quick to point out, before he left town.

"Fish and chips Wow, I can hardly wait," she was silent while she listened intently to the voice on the other end of the line before saying flippantly, "You're all heart," then added more soberly, "Okay, I'll see you shortly."

She turned back to her customer, not quite able to hide the bemused look on her face, or the light sparkle which had infiltrated down into her beautiful hazel eyes.

The Grazier's Proposal

On closer inspection, even with the quick glance he had directed at her, Beale noticed her eyes were flecked with minute pieces of gold dust which were shimmering with anticipation at the arrival of her friend.

He was in little doubt that this person was a man, and it surprised him to find this information left him with a bitter taste in his mouth. He supposed it shouldn't surprise him about her having a boyfriend, or even possibly a string of men, all of whom she kept dangling on a possessive chain, rattling their leads whenever she wanted male company. With those beautiful eyes and long glorious locks of brown hair, he was sure she wouldn't hunger for male company. She would have the poor useless idiots flocking to her in droves, all of them wanting to be the one she would choose to bestow her graciousness upon.

Beale was piqued about the eating arrangements he'd heard her making over the phone. He had planned to ask her if she would like to accompany him out for a bite to eat, feeling it was the least he could do after all the running around she had done for him, buying the bits and pieces that her own shop hadn't stocked. He was certain that not too many proprietors would have gone out of their way for him the way she had, scouring other shops for the items on the list which her shop didn't supply.

He shook his head slightly, trying to rid himself of the image which was manifesting itself in his mind. He was imagining how it would feel to have that soft, supple body pressed firmly against his own muscular contours, to feel the indent of her full, rounded breasts barrelling forcefully into his chest in totally wanton abandonment.

He was therefore disconcerted and slightly embarrassed to find that when he came back to his senses that she was looking enquiringly up at him. Had she spoken to him and he hadn't heard because of his lustful trip into forbidden waters?

"I'm sorry. I was miles away. Did you say something?" he wanted to know as he gazed nonchalantly down at her, belying his thoughts of a few moments ago.

"It wasn't anything important," Peta assured him lightly. She had asked him to whom was the package being given, but one look at his handsome face had said it all. If her guess was correct, he'd been thinking about his wife, or girlfriend. Or both, her wicked mind suggested ruefully.

He was fingering the edges of a wooden photo frame and had been absently caressing the glass, stroking its smoothness over the place where a photo would eventually sit. The simple action had mesmerised Peta, reminding her of a caress which had elevated her heart rate as she watched him carry out this impromptu action.

It was probably best that she didn't know the identity of the recipient of the ribbons and laces, for she couldn't picture the tall willowy blonde sitting down to do arts and craft. Going on this deduction, she concluded they were for someone else. Her mind conjured up a mental picture of a silver haired old lady, probably his grandmother, asking him to pick up these things for her. Yes, that was it, she thought to herself wickedly. The ribbons and laces were for his silver-haired grandmother.

"Well," he said galvanised into action at last, "I must be off. No doubt that phone call will bring results and your boyfriend will be here soon."

Peta opened her mouth to tell him he was mistaken, but something held her back and stilled the words before they left her mouth. She didn't want him to think of her as being dateless and desperate, which she wasn't . . . desperate, that is.

He tipped his hat to her courteously before turning to walk out of the door into the now deserted street. Out of her life forever.

Peta wasn't sure afterwards just what prompted her to follow him, but follow him she did.

"Wait," she called, catching up to him at the corner where he was waiting for the traffic lights to change before he could cross the road.

He turned, looking down at her enquiringly, waiting for her to tell him what she felt was so important that she had chased him halfway down the street.

"I wanted to give you my card just in case you need any more supplies in the future. You can phone me direct, or write, whichever is easiest for you."

"Thank you. I'll keep that in mind. Was there anything else?"

"No," Peta answered lamely, regretting the impetuousness that had caused her to run after him. She slowly retraced her steps, feeling a complete fool for letting her emotions take over like that. The card didn't even have her name on it. It came from a batch that had been made up incorrectly and only had the name and address of the shop written across the front. Peta usually scribbled her name on the back of any cards she gave out, but she realised reluctantly that this card hadn't been signed before it had been so hastily grabbed from under the counter where she kept them.

The panoramic view spread out majestically before Peta normally filled her with awe and a certain amount of vibrant inspiration. The foam-capped waves crashing against the shore with such energetic force had always held a fascination for her, but not today.

Today she sat looking through unseeing eyes which were filled with misery, despair and hopelessness. Her entire world had been turned upside down in a matter of hours. Her brain was still dulled from the shock of it all. She couldn't fully comprehend even now the events of the last twelve hours except to admit to herself that she had lost everything in the world that she owned. All she had left were the clothes she wore, her car and a few bits and pieces which had somehow escaped the ravages of the fire which had so cruelly destroyed the life she had been steadily building for herself.

Faulty wiring, the firefighters had told her, had caused a short in the electrical system and because the building was so old the flames had spread quickly, devouring everything in a matter of minutes. They had told her how lucky she was not to have been in the small flat at the back of the building because then she, too, would have been a statistic losing her life to the flames and smoke.

Peta had gone to the movies, hoping to lift her flagging spirits. Nelson hadn't been able to come with her. He'd had someone he had to meet. She'd purposely picked a movie that was meant to have left her feeling light-hearted and full of remembered laughter. Then she'd seen her mystery man and nearly choked on popcorn. Added to that, to complete her day, a fire had destroyed her business. As a day, she thought it had been a hum-dinger!

The vast jets of water which had been focused on the burning building had literally washed away any stock not destroyed by the flames. It would be a miracle if anything had survived. She certainly wasn't going to sift through the mess until she could see exactly what she was doing. Anyway, the firefighters had forbidden it, telling her it was too dangerous as the walls could collapse. They would prefer it if she could come back later.

She remembered how she had stood helplessly watching as the flames devoured not only her business and her home, but her dreams. That had been hours ago. The firefighters and the police had been very supportive, as had the other tenants of the building. It was only Peta who hadn't been contacted because she'd decided to go out.

Peta spent the next few hours sitting in her car, gazing glassy eyed at the pile of rubble that until a few short hours ago had made up the major part of her life. She was twenty-six years old. Was she now supposed to start her life over again? Doing what, she wondered. Did she have the courage it would take to make a fresh start?

She ran shaking hands through her hair as the full impact of the fire assaulted her senses. Nostalgia for times past filled her heart. She suddenly felt so tired, so deflated, and a dull depression seemed to permeate throughout every cell in her body. Fighting back an impulse to burst into tears, she whispered brokenly, "Oh Nan, how I wish you were here with me now. I really need you."

Driving to the beach in the early hours of the morning, Peta found herself drawn to one of her favourite spots. She had come upon this lonely stretch of beach on one of her many jaunts to the coast and had since visited the area many times. The natural beauty and tranquillity which pervaded the area always captivated her imagination. One day, she thought she'd like to capture its beauty on canvas. Local people had told her that this area bordered onto the state forest which was directly behind her, but on this clear, crisp pre-dawn morning none of the beauty touched her. It was as if she was in mourning all over again.

This was the time of day that Peta loved best. The earth was waiting to be touched by the sun. It was having a glorious effect on the wildlife in the area. Birds were waking up and were chirping noisily in the tall trees, which marked the boundary of the state forest adjoining the sandy stretch of beach. Their chorus rose above the gentle lapping of the waves, which caressed the sand in front of her bare feet.

A dull depression had settled over her as she wondered what she would do with her life. How was she going to live, to support herself? All of her available assets had been tied up in the shop. She was fully insured, but that wouldn't help her immediate future. The bit of money she had wouldn't last long. Also, where would she live? She was forced to give a rueful smile as she envisaged herself living in her car here on the beach.

Almost against her will, the tears flowed. Slowly at first and then with a scalding urgency which left her face stained from the soot and smoke which she hadn't bothered to wipe away. Drawing her legs up into her chest, Peta forlornly laid her head onto her knees, hugging them tightly with her arms as she gave in to the tears that racked her body. She didn't know how long she cried and wasn't aware that she had company until she heard footsteps crunching in the bracken behind her.

Hearing a male voice saying hello to her, Peta knew instantly that it belonged to her mystery man. Afraid to turn around and face him, she quickly wiped the tears away with hands that weren't altogether steady. Her emotions were anything but stable and she didn't relish the thought of talking to anyone, let alone him. She had driven to this spot to be alone. She hoped he would take the hint and leave her alone.

Unaware of her inner turmoil, Beale hunkered down onto his haunches beside her. He'd been out for an early morning run along the beach when he'd noticed the silhouette of someone outlined against the early morning sky. There had been something vaguely familiar about the figure which had drawn him closer, wanting a better look, making him change direction and head over towards her, for he was sure it was a female who sat huddled up on the beach. He wasn't going to pass her by until he knew what was going on. He'd be darned if he was going to let her fob him off this time. His intuition told him something was wrong. Why would she be here otherwise!

"What brings you out here at the crack of dawn?" he wanted to know as he scrutinised her face, noticing the tremendous effort she was making not to appear upset in front of him. He noticed the dirt and grime on her face and her unkempt appearance, which brought a tight knot to his stomach as his mind tried to search for a logical reason for her being here, in this bedraggled state.

He had left her yesterday after picking up the package for his mother, looking forward to a visit from a friend. What had happened between then and now that had reduced her to this quivering mess?

Reaching out a bronzed hand, he slowly and gently put his fingers under her chin, turning her face around so that he could look her squarely in the eyes. Her eyes were red and swollen, which was a dead giveaway to him she had been crying.

"What's happened? Who did this to you?" he wanted to know. His voice held a quiet authority, which demanded an immediate answer. She appeared to be in shock, so he tried to be patient, but he was determined that his questions would be answered. He prayed that his fears about her so-called friend attacking her were without foundation, but if that turned out to be the case. His hands formed tight fists as he waited for her to answer him. This was the only outward sign which showed that he was seethingly angry and very alarmed by her deliberate silence.

Peta recognised the command in his voice, but she could also detect a gentleness lying beneath the surface to which she could respond.

"N . . . nothing," she stammered feebly, "No one has hurt me. I . . . I . . . ," Peta felt the tears starting to flow once more and lowered her head onto her knees trying to get away from his probing green-eyed stare.

"What then. Tell me. Perhaps I can help."

"No one can help. It's too late," Peta hiccuped, staring at the ground, remembering the charred remains of her business and home.

"Maybe, but let me be the judge of that, okay," he told her then added, "Troubles are always better when you share them with someone, don't you think. Anyway, we've been through too many adventures already. I feel as if I know you." he eased himself down on to the grass beside Peta, letting her know with this gesture that he would not leave until she told him the reason for her tears.

Peta smiled despite herself. They did have a habit of bumping into each other. How many times had it been now, four. She brokenly told him about the fire, about coming back from the movies to find she had nothing, not even a bed to sleep in.

"I came down here to think. I come here a lot when I have the time." It didn't occur to her to ask him why he was here, how he had appeared out of nowhere and walked into her life once more when she had most needed a shoulder to lean on.

When she had finished talking, he remained silent for so long Peta raised her tear-stained face to look up at him. He was regarding her thoughtfully, almost as if he was trying to make a decision of some sort.

"Anyway," Peta added, talking with a bravado which she was far from feeling, "I should be going. I need to go back and sift through the rubble, if that's at all possible. I guess I'll have to find a place to stay as well until I decide what I'm going to do. Thank you for listening. You're right, troubles are better shared." Fresh tears sprang into her eyes, and she wiped them away with a trembling hand. She made a move to get up, feeling as if she had encroached upon this man's time for far too long.

It therefore surprised Peta when he pulled her back down onto the grass beside him. She turned tear-stained eyes towards him, wondering what was happening.

"You're in no fit state to go anywhere. You don't have to leave or try to put on a brave face for me or for anyone else, for that matter. If you want to cry, there's no better place to do it than right here." He patted his shoulder, letting her know in no uncertain terms that he didn't mind if she used him, if she wanted a shoulder to cry on.

Peta turned into his shoulder and sobbed uncontrollably. Her body was racked with the pain of losing everything she had worked so hard to build over the past year. She felt his strong arms go around her and knew instinctively that it was a gesture of comfort, nothing else. She felt safe here in his arms and for the moment didn't want to be anywhere else.

While Peta cried, Beale thought of the shop she had lost and how hard she had probably worked to make it the success he thought it to be. He remembered looking around while she had been out the back and while he hadn't been particularly interested in the items he saw around him, he could see how much time and effort she had put into making it the kind of establishment where customers would feel welcome and be encouraged to come back.

He was also very much aware of the woman he held in his arms. He could feel her body pressed into his and had to fight the urge which was spreading throughout his traitorous body to plant small sweet kisses along her neck and jawline. She trusted him and he would not break that trust, not for a quick moment of passion. She needed him, and he planned to be there for her for the duration. The only thing was, he had to convince her of that.

Peta's sobs subsided after a while, but she was reluctant to move away from him. She knew she must, for there was no way she could vindicate staying securely wrapped in his arms the way she was. Pushing herself slowly away from his strong, warm body, she felt slightly embarrassed and wasn't sure of just what she should say to him.

The matter was taken out of her hands when he looked down into her face and said smilingly, "There, what did I tell you. You must feel a bit better. I know you've still got a long way to go, but it helps to have a friend hanging around the place sometimes, just in case you need them."

Peta knew he was right. She did feel a lot better, but it still didn't solve the problem of where she was going to stay.

Beale pushed himself up off the ground and then stretched a hand out towards Peta so that he could help her up as well. "Come with me and have some breakfast. My guess is you could use a good strong cup of coffee about now," he hesitated for a few seconds before adding, "I just might be able to help you out of your current predicament, and you might be able to help me out of mine."

Peta was sitting at the kitchen table, watching Beale as he deftly moved around the room. She had showered and changed into one of his t-shirts and a pair of his jeans. Both items of clothing were far too big for her, but she had to admit that she felt much better for having had a wash. She had helped herself to the shampoo and conditioner which had been on the ledge by the bathtub, then had used some deodorant she had found nearby. She had also sprinkled a small amount of aftershave over herself, deciding she liked the aroma that permeated the air when she had finished. She had started to relax, but her sleepless night plus the shock of losing all of her belongings was taking its toll on her. She was feeling exhausted and knew that before long she'd have to find a motel where she could have a sleep before working out where she would go from here.

"Do you live here?" Peta asked as she tried to eat the food which had been placed in front of her. She had completely forgotten their conversation from earlier in the week when he'd told her he'd be leaving Rockhampton on Sunday. Today was Sunday.

"No, it belongs to my family. We use it as a holiday home whenever we come to the coast, which isn't very often," he told her as he joined her at the kitchen table.

"Oh, where is home then?" she asked, trying to make polite conversation as they ate their meal. She was afraid that if they stopped talking, the silence between them would be deafening.

"What's this ... twenty questions? This is the most you've ever said to me. It has to be some sort of a record." He threw her a lop-sided grin from his side of the table, and it made Peta very aware of his sparkling green eyes as he looked across at her.

"I'm sorry," Peta replied. She could feel her face flaming, and she was engulfed with embarrassment that

The Grazier's Proposal

he'd thought it necessary to curb the questions she was asking him. A bright sheen covered her eyes, and she turned her attention once more to the plate of food in front of her.

Beale could have kicked himself for upsetting her. It was the last thing he wanted to do. He reached across the table and patted one of her hands.

"Hey, it's alright," he told her, then frowned suddenly as a thought occurred to him, "Do you know something; we still don't know each other's name. We must both be suffering from a terrible lack of curiosity."

Peta looked at him, her eyes very solemn, wondering if she should go first or should she let him introduce himself as it was he who had brought up the subject of names.

He raised his eyebrows as he gazed across at her expectantly, waiting for her to tell him her name. "Well," he finally prompted when he realised she wasn't going to be forthcoming with her name of her own accord.

"It's Jupiter Masters, but everyone calls me Peta."

"Jupiter, it's very unusual, but I like it. I think I'll call you Jupiter. How do you do, Jupiter Masters, my name is Beale Jacobs. I'm very pleased to meet you." Upon saying this, he held his hand out to her across the table and Peta put her own small hand into his. She liked the way her hand seemed to fit comfortably into his much larger one. The tingle of delight which raced spontaneously along her nerve endings and throughout her body at the contact between them surprised her.

"Hello Beale," she said shyly, feeling very tongue tired and therefore couldn't think of a thing to say which could be added to their rather one sided conversation.

"Hello," he replied, smiling across at her, knowing full well the response was totally unnecessary.

In any other circumstances, that smile would have completely overwhelmed Peta. It lit up his entire face, making his green eyes sparkle and dance, but all she could muster was a stifled yawn. She felt embarrassed because he was being so nice, giving her comfort when really, except for a few chance meetings, she was still very much a perfect stranger. The events of the last twelve hours were catching up with her, and she felt weary beyond belief.

"I must be going. If I don't find somewhere to sleep soon, I'll have to sleep in the car and I don't want to do that," Peta told him, trying to hide another yawn. She felt a growing reluctance, which was tinged with regret now that it was time to leave. She found she liked her mystery man, probably a lot more than she cared to admit.

"Sleep here," he told her calmly and then added, "there's plenty of room and if you remember, I wanted to talk to you. I can't very well do that if you leave, can I. Anyway, you're wearing my clothes. How were you proposing to get them back to me?"

He was smiling as he said this last bit letting Peta know he didn't care in the least if he never saw his t-shirt and jeans again, but her mind had caught on his suggestion that she stay here with him, at least for now.

"Here, I can't. I've put you out enough for one day. No, no, I don't think so," Peta stammered, nonplused by his suggestion. Apprehension shot through her as she looked across at him.

Sensing her thoughts, he interjected quickly, "Hold on, Jupiter. You've got it all wrong. I don't have any ulterior motives here, like trying to get you into bed. I was offering you a place to stay, that's all. Surely by now you know you can trust me, don't you?"

She found herself relaxing. It would be nice to stay here with him, at least for today. She could find somewhere else later, when she felt more refreshed.

"I don't want to put you out," she told him feebly as she tried to hide yet another yawn.

Despite being so tired, her body was responding to him, to his nearness. She felt inexplicably drawn to this man. He affected her like no other man before him.

"You're not. Now come on, off to bed, you're dead on your feet. I have to go out so if you're worried about me lurking about the place you can put your mind at rest, okay."

"It's not that," Peta tried to tell him. She couldn't believe how incredibly tired she felt. Her body was literally shutting down. Her eyelids hung heavily, almost obliterating her eyes while her body felt lethargic to the point where she found it difficult to move. She stood up, intending to walk away from the table, but almost immediately felt herself pitching forward and would have fallen to the floor if not for Beale's lightning movements. He caught her in his arms before picking her up and carrying her from the room.

"Right, that's settled. You're going to bed, now! No arguments. You'll be perfectly safe, so don't worry." Beale carried her effortlessly through to the back of the house, down a short hallway to a bedroom where he laid her gently onto a bed which felt so comfortable Peta almost immediately descended into sleep. The last thing she remembered was Beale standing over her, almost like a sentinel guarding his princess. A look of concern dominated his features, but Peta thought she detected something else. At the moment that something else eluded her as her body gave in to the sleep which she'd been keeping at bay for so many hours.

Chapter Three

PETA WOKE SOME TIME later and was momentarily disorientated by her strange surroundings. The room she found herself in was light, airy, and quite large. The furnishings were old, but of a good quality, having stood the test of time. The bed was a large four poster and Peta stretched luxuriously, loving the way the mattress seemed to engulf her in its softness. The furniture belonged to another era, one that was long since past; an era that had probably flourished long before her grandmother's time. Peta loved the pieces and looked around her with interest. She would have liked to have had the time to look at them in more detail.

Despite her current dilemma, Peta wondered about the people who had occupied the house prior to its current owners. Did Beale have a blood connection to its background?

The house was old, nestled amongst the trees of the forest. A large canopy of trees completely screened it on all sides. The only way to the outside world was via a private road which wound its way through the trees, making the house very secluded indeed. She would have to ask him about its history. Would he answer her or fob her off as he had done this morning?

She barely remembered being carried to the bedroom, but had felt instead a feeling of strength and security surrounding her. Strong arms had held her close to a warm, vibrant body where she had felt the steady beat of Beale's heart, as her head had rested heavily against his muscular chest. Just as her mind had bordered on the verge of sleep, she was sure that he had gently stroked her forehead, crooning words of encouragement to her to go to sleep, that she was safe.

She certainly felt a lot better now that she had rested and the smell of food being cooked reached her nostrils, reminding her she hadn't eaten a proper meal in quite a while. She had toyed with the breakfast which had been placed before her earlier in the day, but hadn't been able to swallow more than a few small mouthfuls. Now hunger was gnawing at her, but she wondered if she should venture out of her safe haven to make her way towards the kitchen. The decision was taken out of her hands as she heard footsteps coming down the wooden hallway towards the room where she lay.

"So you're awake at last. Do you feel like something to eat?" Beale asked her pleasantly. He didn't enter the room, but stood instead in the doorway, waiting for her reply.

Peta had the distinct impression that he had looked in on her prior to her waking. She wasn't sure if she was comfortable with the fact that he'd been watching her sleep. It made her feel vulnerable somehow, and she wasn't sure she liked feeling this way where he was concerned. The trouble is, she told herself, you like him and you're scared that you might let your feelings show. He's just being kind helping you out and here you are thinking about his incredibly sexy green eyes and his lean muscular body.

She sat up, swinging her legs over the side of the bed. As usual with him, she had lost the power of speech and couldn't think of anything intelligent to say. She thought of her last fiasco at the breakfast table and vowed she would try to keep away from questions of a personal nature. Searching her brain, she wasn't able to come up with a single subject that she thought would interest him.

She finally answered in a small voice, telling him simply, "That would be nice. It smells delicious. What time is it anyway? Have I slept for very long?"

"Okay, well, when you're ready, come along to the kitchen. As for the time, you've slept for most of the day. It's . . . ,"

He got no further as Peta exclaimed, "Oh no! I had to go back to the shop. There were things to be done. I have to go. I told the police I'd be there to see them this morning to sort everything out with them. They'll be wondering what happened to me." Peta looked frantically around the room for her things. Drat this man, she thought wildly, why hadn't he woken her? He knew this was important to her. Here she was thinking he cared about her well-being. Well, he probably does in some small way, she amended, but he obviously doesn't understand.

Beale raised his hand, gesturing for her to stop talking and to listen to him. He purposely held back from telling her the shop and the small apartment had been totally demolished by the fire. He doubted if she'd find anything of value, if she was to rake through the ashes. The entire building had been destroyed, and the authorities had roped the area off pending an investigation into the likely cause of the incident. He was sure the area would be safe from vandals. Anyway, he wanted to be with her if she started rummaging through the debris. He felt a protective urge surge through him as he looked down at her. He didn't want her to be hurt any more.

"It's alright. I took the liberty of going around there while I was in town today. I gave the police this address so they know where you are and how to contact you if they need to. If you still want to go, you can do so after you've eaten." He had taken command of the situation once again, and Peta was secretly relieved to have him do this for her. He had told her earlier that he wanted to discuss something with her, but as yet he had remained silent, not saying what that something was.

"Look," he continued as he looked down at her from where he stood framed in the doorway, "they gave me a phone number, if you want to phone them to find out for yourself just how bad the damage is, feel free, but for now come and eat before everything gets cold. The bathroom's through there if you want to wash up before dinner." Upon saying this, he spun on his heel to return down the hallway towards the kitchen.

"Good one, Peta," she chastised herself when she was once again alone in the room. The problem was, she admitted to herself, she did trust him, but where was it going to get her. She did appreciate the fact that he had been on hand to help her when she had most needed help. She was going to have to tell him that she was thankful for his help, but for some reason, she found it difficult to relate to him. She found herself wishing that Nelson was here with her, sharing her hardship. Things were so uncomplicated with him. They were just good friends, and he always knew what to do, and at least with him she was never tongue tired. He was always complaining that she talked too much. She looked once more around the room, noticing that long shadows were starting to make their way through the open window, telling her she had indeed slept the day away.

Peta smiled when she heard him calling her. He certainly didn't stand on ceremony. "Jupiter, come and eat before everything gets cold."

"Coming," she yelled back as she walked out of the room. She vowed she'd take an active role in the conversation.

The jeans she wore were rolled halfway up her legs and were held up with one of his belts which had needed another hole punched into it to stop them from slipping down over her slim hips. She felt self-conscious as she entered the kitchen, feeling like a waif. He was serving their evening meal, and she had to admit that it really smelled delicious.

"Do you do a lot of cooking," she asked him. Now here was a nice, safe topic which they could explore.

"Only out of necessity when I'm saving fire ravaged maidens," he answered as he placed a plate of food in front of her.

"Are you on holiday?" she asked as she took a mouthful of food, pleasantly surprised that it tasted as good as it smelt.

He interpreted her look of surprise and sent her a lop-sided grin before he answered her question. "No, strictly business, but I might change my mind and take a few days off."

"Hold on," Peta said as she glanced across at him. A thought had just occurred to her. She remembered their conversation from earlier in the week. "Weren't you supposed to be leaving today? Didn't you tell me you were leaving Sunday? Unless I've slept longer than I think I have, today is Sunday!" She fervently hoped that her untimely arrival on the scene this morning hadn't stopped him from carrying out his plans to leave for home, wherever home might be.

"You've got a good memory. I was going to leave today, yes, but I've changed my mind." He didn't offer any more information, making Peta feel guilty knowing that she was probably the cause of his late departure. She hoped there wasn't anyone who was waiting patiently, and lovingly, for him to arrive home.

"What exactly is it you do?" Peta wanted to know. She thought he had something to do with the land and was therefore not surprised by his answer.

"I work on a cattle property. It's a fair way from here. I was driving in that day; it seems so long ago now, doesn't it? My car broke down. I'm still waiting for a part then I can start back." He didn't tell her that someone else could have driven the car out to the property, that he had purposely waited around Rockhampton hoping to see her again. Instead he told her, "I'm checking out the cattle sales while I'm here, so all isn't lost."

"Getting in good with the boss," Peta inquired flippantly as she looked across at him.

"I am the boss," he told her simply.

"Oh," was all Peta could think of to say to this particular admission.

"Marry you!" Peta echoed his words in disbelief, wondering why a man as charismatic as Beale Jacobs would want to ask a woman to marry him after such a brief acquaintance, and under such bizarre circumstances. Actually, if Peta was to be honest with herself, she couldn't even class herself as an acquaintance because after their initial meeting by the side of the road their meetings had come about purely by chance and then they'd only lasted a few minutes, not even long enough to utter a per functionary greeting before each had moved on.

"You don't have to make it sound like a death sentence," Beale shot back at her, clearly stung by her astonished outburst. He wasn't sure what reaction his proposal of marriage would bring, but he'd been hoping that she would say yes.

"Beale, please, it's not that. I just didn't expect a marriage proposal with my coffee, that's all." She hoped her explanation would pacify him. She continued in a calmer state of mind, "I don't understand, why a marriage proposal, and why me?"

"I can see I've stunned you. Can you bear with me while I explain the rather bizarre circumstances I find myself in? Would you like to go for a walk along the beach?" Taking control of the situation, Beale stood up, taking it for granted that Peta would automatically follow, which she did.

Beale didn't speak again until they were on the beach. The moonlight was playing over the gently lapping waves, giving them a mystical appearance. Peta thought she'd take her cue from Beale. She'd wait for him to speak, for goodness knows she'd lost her tongue. The thought of marrying Beale was flying around in her head, jamming itself into every cell her fevered brain possessed. What would her answer be? He'd said earlier that she'd benefit from the marriage. What did he mean by that remark?

Beale broke into her thoughts by suddenly asking her, "Do you have any family, Jupiter?"

"No, my grandmother died eighteen months ago. She was the only family I had. My parents died when I was fifteen."

"I'm sorry, but in a way you're lucky," he told her with a tinge of bitterness in his voice.

"Lucky, how do you conclude that?" Peta still missed her grandmother terribly. They had been very close, despite the vast difference in their ages.

"It doesn't matter. What does matter is why I asked you to marry me."

"So it wasn't a joke then?" Peta said, trying to bring a touch of spontaneity to the moment.

"No, it wasn't a joke," he told her soberly, "far from it. The fact is, Jupiter, I need a wife, someone who will come back to the property with me and set up house."

"Well, when you put it like that, how could I refuse," she smiled across at him and saw the ghost of a smile flit across his taut features, "Perhaps if you were to explain, to use your own words, the rather bizarre circumstances you're in, I'd be able to make a decision based on what I know rather than what I'm thinking."

"And just what are you thinking?" he wanted to know, spurred on by her rather odd behaviour. She was certainly surprising him. It was as if she was coming out of her shell, blossoming before his very eyes. Perhaps she wasn't the shy young thing he took her to be.

Peta took her time in answering. She didn't want to say the wrong thing to this man. She couldn't explain her erratic behaviour. Perhaps it was the moonlight, perhaps it was delayed shock. She had heard that shock could manifest itself in several ways. She took a deep breath before plunging on. "I think you're not the type of man who has to ask a complete stranger if she will marry him, therefore there has to be more to this proposal than meets the eye."

"Well, you're correct in that assumption. Having just lost your own business, Jupiter, you can see how devastating it was for you to lose everything you've poured your entire life into and quite possibly your heart?"

Yes, she had been devastated and was still reeling from the loss. Was that why she was considering this weird marriage proposal, because even though she hadn't given him an answer in so many words, her mind was indeed considering how it would feel to be Mrs. Beale Jacobs.

He continued, not expecting an answer, "I'm the fifth generation to take over the running of Blackrock Downs.

The power has passed down from father to son for all of that time. My father is dead, but my mother is still alive. Now that dad is gone, she prefers to live away from the main house. I had a small cottage built for her about five kilometres away. She seems to be happy there. Too many memories, perhaps. She doesn't talk about the past very much, and I don't invade her privacy on the matter. She told me once that the house was for me and my family and no amount of talking could get her to change her mind on the subject."

"It sounds like she has a strong will. It's nice to know that some women still have a mind of their own and can make their own decisions about things that concern them." Peta thought she would like Beale's mother if she ever had the chance to meet her. She continued as a thought struck her, "Does your mother have anything to do with your needing to get married, Beale?"

"In a roundabout way, yes," Beale answered her, "I seem to be making a complete hash of all of this when all I wanted to do was try to simplify things for you. I've made it more of a mystery than before."

"Perhaps," Peta agreed. Her curiosity was well and truly aroused. "Sometimes it's better to just blurt things out and then go over them at a more leisurely pace afterwards. I think you should do that, Beale."

Almost as if the decision had been made for him Beale said, "When my father died there was a clause in his will stating that if I wasn't married by the time I was thirty-five the property would go to the nearest living relative who was married."

"But that's archaic!" Peta was stunned. She exclaimed, "Surely you can get your father's will overturned in a court of law. A request of that nature seems almost ridiculous."

"I've spent the last twelve months trying to do just that, but it seems my father was adamant and his will is ironclad. It has something to do with his not wanting me to live my life in solitude and so forth. If I fail to marry by the end of next month, and produce an heir by the first anniversary, Blackrock goes to some idiot living in Perth. I can assure you I'm not going to let that happen."

"Did you say produce an heir!" Peta could feel the hairs on the back of her neck standing on edge. To marry him was one thing, but to have his child, to live with him as his wife in every sense of the word was something completely different. She didn't miss the tightly controlled anger which flowed beneath the surface of his words. To lose everything because of a clause in a will, to be forced to marry against his will, to live with someone as his wife, how galling it must be for someone like Beale who, she could see, was very much used to making up his own mind about matters which related to his own life. How it must have tortured him to have to ask her to be his wife. She almost felt sorry for him.

When he didn't answer her query, she looked across at him through the darkness and her heart went out to him. She could see he was fighting back the bitterness that was building up in him.

"Should I be flattered that you've asked me, or are you just running out of time?" she wanted to know.

He smiled despite himself. He was learning more about this woman with every passing minute, and he found he liked the things he was learning about her. She had a sense of humour, which appealed to him.

"Oh, I had another card up my sleeve, one I'm sure I could have pulled out in the nick of time if I had to." This statement deflated Peta's ego as she thought once more about the beautiful blonde she'd seen Beale escorting to the cinema. She wondered idly how the blonde woman would respond to Beale's proposal of marriage. She was sure she would have answered in the affirmative, but what about a child? Would she have wanted to spoil that beautiful, shapely body by becoming pregnant? Perhaps Beale had already asked her, and she had turned him down. Perhaps she'd broken his heart. The thought of Beale nursing a broken heart, pinning over another woman, didn't bear thinking about.

She said simply, "What if I'm unable to produce an heir in the prescribed amount of time?" It was a very real possibility, and one they would both have to live with if she couldn't conceive a child. She felt like a prize heifer and wondered sadly if she'd be sold off if she couldn't fulfill her part of the bargain. Would he try again with someone else? Had he already tried with someone else and failed? Images of the blonde woman came unbidden into her mind, and she flicked a hand across her brow to rid herself of the disturbing image of Beale with the other woman.

"We'll cross that bridge when we come to it. The main thing is that you understand that if you agree to become my wife, it won't be a marriage in name only. I need a wife, Jupiter, not a name on a piece of paper."

"I'm not a child, Beale. I understand exactly what it is you are saying. You'll require me to make love with you should I agree to marry you on these terms." Peta hoped he couldn't hear the tremble in her voice as she told him she understood the situation she would be placing herself in.

"Yes." His face was a closed book as he looked at her, so she wasn't able to hazard any kind of guess what he must be thinking.

"Blackrock Downs must mean a lot to you if you're prepared to go to these lengths to save it," she asked him quietly.

"Blackrock has been a part of my family for five generations. I'm not about to give up without a fight. I think you'll grow to like it out there, Jupiter," he told her simply.

Peta sat silently for the next few minutes before she told Beale simply, "If you don't mind, I think I'll go to bed. You've given me a lot to think about. Also, if you remember, I have to go into town tomorrow to sort out any belongings that weren't destroyed by the fire . . . ," after a pause she added, "some bride I'm going to make, I won't even have a dowry."

"I hadn't forgotten about the fire and as for the dowry, you won't need one." It elated Beale to hear her speaking positively about marrying him. It meant that she hadn't totally discarded the idea as completely ludicrous.

They walked back to the house in silence, but Peta had been nagged by harrowing thoughts which she had to get off her chest and there was one question she knew she had to ask before she gave the matter any more consideration.

"Beale," she said, stopping him as he was about to head through the door which lead back out to the verandah.

He turned to look at her with inquiring eyes, waiting for her question.

Taking her pride and throwing it away she asked, "If I hadn't turned up here this morning having lost everything I possessed, would you have given me a second thought, or was asking me just a spur-of-the-moment thing that you might come to regret in the morning?"

"There are a lot of things I regret, Jupiter, but meeting you hasn't been one of them so you can put your mind to rest. I admit your turning up here this morning was a stroke of luck for me. I know I can't replace what you've lost, but maybe I can offer you something to take their place. You'll never have to worry about material things again if you agree to this marriage. Now run along to bed. You look dead on your feet. We'll talk more in the morning." He dismissed her as if she was a child and Peta went, glad to be alone with her thoughts. She realised they did have a lot to talk about. She wanted answers to so many questions.

After Peta had gone to bed, Beale headed for the kitchen, where he made himself a last cup of coffee. He wasn't sure what to make of the situation he found himself in. She had asked him if he would have given her a second thought. Heavens, she was practically all he had thought about since he'd walked into her shop the other day. He had wanted to ask her out to dinner last night. God, was it only last night. So much had happened in such a short space of time, but that phone call she'd received had knocked that thought on the head. He wondered where that caller was now; did he have a permanent place in her heart and if so, why didn't she go to him? He found he didn't care. All he knew was that she was here with him and that he had asked her to marry him. He prayed God would take pity on him and let her final answer be yes. Was it possible to fall in love in such a short space of time? A few days ago he would have said no, but now he wasn't so sure.

Peta spent a restless night turning over in her mind the reasons she shouldn't marry Beale Jacobs, but for every valid reason her tormented brain came up with, she could make a legitimate excuse of some description, turning her negative response into an affirmative answer.

From the very first moment she had set eyes on this man, he had disturbed her thoughts. She hadn't been able to completely erase him from her mind, or from her memory. A pair of flashing green eyes and hair the colour of ravens wings had haunted her dreams over the past week, making it impossible for her to think of anything else. And now here she was, a guest in his home because of a catastrophe in her own life. He was offering her a way out of her immediate problems, but, her mind tried to reason with her, don't you think a lifelong commitment tied to him is taking thank you just a little too far. Wouldn't it be easier to merely shake his hand and be on your way?

The thought of not being able to see him again was probably the catalyst for Peta's decision, for when she tried to picture her life without him in it, she felt truly empty and alone. There are some decisions in life; she told herself that have to be made promptly. Sometimes, if you wait, everything can be lost. She didn't know why exactly, but she felt this was one of those times. She prayed with all of her heart that she was making the right decision, because it wasn't just her own life's happiness that was at stake here, but Beale's as well.

She told Beale the next morning that she would marry him. She was pleased to see his face fill with an emotion akin to relief.

"This calls for a celebration, but I'm sorry to say there's not a drop of alcohol in the place. I've been meaning to restock the shelf. Will you settle for a cup of coffee until later? I'll take you out to lunch so we can celebrate. How about it?"

"That sounds fine, but have you forgotten I've got nothing to wear." Peta drew his attention to the clothes she was wearing, his clothes.

"You look fine to me," he told her, then added with a silly grin plastered on his face, "Is this what it means when your future wife tells you she has nothing to wear?"

"I don't think so, no. Can you be serious for a minute? I can't very well go into town looking like this, can I?" She did a quick pirouette in front of him. The t-shirt she wore was definitely oversized and hung loosely from her slim shoulders. The short sleeves reached way below her elbows and the jeans were held up with one of his belts, which could have gone twice around her slim waist. Even then the bottoms had to be rolled up a few times before they were the correct length.

"Damn, I wish I had some cl . . . . Hey! Wait a minute! I do have some clothes." Peta's face lit up as she remembered the clothes in the boot of her car. She raced outside, followed closely by Beale, who wondered what was going on.

Unlocking the boot of her car, she told him excitedly. "Clothes, wonderful clothes. I forgot I went to the Laundromat on Friday night after closing the shop. I was so tired I left them in the boot. I was going to get them out yesterday. I guess it's a good thing I didn't." She finished on a quieter note as memories came flooding back to haunt her about the shop and everything she'd lost.

"Life certainly has some funny twists and turns, doesn't it," she mused as she made her way back upstairs, following Beale as he carried the basket of clothes into her bedroom.

Beale nodded, realising she really didn't want an answer, but was merely thinking aloud.

Sitting down on the bed next to her basket of clothes, Peta looked across the short expanse of the bedroom to the man who was shortly going to be her husband. He was leaning easily against a chest of drawers, supporting himself comfortably on one elbow.

"What?" he wanted to know, puzzled by her thoughtful expression, which was being directed at him.

"I was just wondering about the man I'm about to marry. I know nothing about you other than the fact that you need a wife. I know we touched on it briefly last night, but I'd seriously like to know what your plans were. How were you going to go about it? What would you have done if you couldn't find anyone crazy enough to fall in with your plans? Does the fact that I've said yes give me the right to know what your plans were going to be?"

"Yes, you have every right to know. We're going to be partners in this marriage, Jupiter. That means no secrets on both sides."

Peta thought of the blonde woman, but kept her own counsel as to whom she might be. Instead, she looked up at him, nervously expectant, as she waited for the answers to her questions.

"Over the past year or so as I've already told you, I've been trying to overturn my father's will, but I've also taken out a few women occasionally hoping I'd meet someone who attracted me enough that I'd want to make one of them my wife. Suffice to say, none of them measured up to my expectations of what a grazier's wife should be."

"Then you met me. I was a prime candidate because of my situation," she told him levelly. Where else could he have found someone who fitted the bill so perfectly? She was practically destitute and in desperate need of somewhere to stay. He probably knew she'd say yes to his proposal. Women married every day for security, rather than wait for love, but she had never thought in her wildest dreams that she would be one of those women. She knew she wanted to marry one day, to raise a family of her own, but she had always thought she'd be in love . . .

"No!" he shot at her with such vehemence that she visibly jumped, frightened out of her reverie by the sharpness of his voice. "That's not true. I asked you because I liked you and I honestly thought we could help each other out. We're both in this for the long haul. It's important that we like each other. I've known marriages to fall apart that were based solely on love. Being in love doesn't guarantee a marriage will be an instant success.

Who's to say love won't come later as a natural extension of our liking each other . . . ," he threw her a sheepish look as a thought occurred to him and he asked her suddenly, wanting to know, "Do you like me, Jupiter?"

Peta laughed gleefully at the uncertainty that she saw etched on his handsome features. She was quick to ease his mind. "Yes, I like you. I couldn't go through with this marriage if there wasn't an inkling of some feeling for you. I don't believe in divorce, Beale, so it's important for me too that we succeed at this."

"Good, that's what I like to hear. A positive attitude. Hopefully, when we're old and gray and all of this is behind us, we'll wonder what all the fuss was about. Remind me to tell you sometime about my forebears and how they chose their wives. In light of our situation, I think you'll find it very interesting. In a way, I'm carrying on a family tradition, almost."

Peta threw him a questioning glance, but he wouldn't be drawn out about his ancestors, so she asked him instead, "What if I'd said no, or even worse, what if I turned out to be a gold digger just out for everything I could get? You don't really know me."

"I've been a fairly good judge of character in the past. I don't think you have it in you to be a gold digger, Jupiter. As for the other, you'd have broken my heart."

Peta smiled across at him and she knew she could believe the sincerity in his voice, not about breaking his heart, he'd been joking about that, of course, hadn't he?

"How do you know I'll measure up," she asked him, then added, "What if I let you down?"

He continued in a lighter vein as he told her, "The thought of putting an ad in the personal columns for a potential mate didn't have any appeal. But that would have been my next move if you'd turned me down. Heaven knows who I would have met that way." A frown passed over his features as he contemplated the outcome of such an action.

But instead you ended up with me, she thought to herself. "You were that desperate, Beale?" she asked him sadly. Her heart ached for him, and she promised herself there and then that she would do everything in her power to make their marriage a success.

She continued, "So that's why you were coming into Rockhampton that day, to find a suitable woman, one who would eventually become your wife?"

"You make it sound so cold-hearted when you put it like that. You've saved me from a fate worse than death," he winced at the memory, then added, telling her, "I had a meeting with my solicitor and I caught up with an old friend."

Peta wondered if the old friend was the blond woman from the other night, but said nothing. Instead she asked him, "I wonder if you'll be saying that in forty years' time."

They both laughed and Beale, on an impulse, reached for her, pulling her to her feet. He planted a quick, firm kiss on her lips.

"Mmm, that was nice," he told her pleasantly, looking down to see her reaction to the meeting of their lips.

"Yes," she agreed, totally unprepared for the tingling sensation which was still, even now, coursing throughout her body, filling her with excited anticipation.

"Would you like to try that again?" he wanted to know, all laughter now gone from his face. Instead, it had been replaced by a more compelling, more serious expression as he gazed down into her upturned face. He was holding her loosely within the circle of his arms, letting her know with his eyes that if she wanted to break the contact between them, then all she had to do was step away from him. It would be that easy.

She merely nodded, not able to trust her voice, but she took a step closer to him, letting him know by her action that she, too, had been moved by the simple kiss they'd shared.

"You're so sweet," Beale whispered just before their lips met, "So very sweet."

Peta could feel the fire dancing through her veins as their kiss deepened, and she pressed herself even closer to Beale's body, feeling the hard strength of him against the supple softness of her own. His kisses were everything she could have wished for. She found herself responding to his special brand of charm without the slightest bit of hesitation.

When at last their lips parted, Peta found she was embarrassed, and Beale looked down at her suspiciously when she wouldn't meet his eyes.

"Peta, are you alright?" he put long fingers under her chin raising her crimson tinged face so he could look at her more closely.

"You called me Peta," she told him self-consciously.

"So I did. I think Jupiter has gone forever. She's been replaced by her very sexy counterpart."

"No one has ever thought of me as sexy before," she told him truthfully.

"They don't know what they're missing."

Sometime later, while they were sitting on the verandah drinking a last cup of coffee before heading into town for lunch, Peta tentatively broached a subject to Beale that had been troubling her. After all, the entire basis for their marriage was so that they could produce an heir together, saving Beale's inheritance, not only for himself, but for any future generations that might follow.

"Beale," she began, only to find that her voice broke from sheer nervousness. She cleared her throat and began again. "Beale, do you, um, that is, would you like me to have a fertility test to make sure that I'm able to conceive a child?"

"What?" the question had taken Beale completely by surprise.

"I said do you want . . . ," she got no further, for Beale quickly interrupted her. He was quick to see the grave concern etched on her brow, causing deep furrows to rest there. On a sudden impulse he reached for her hand, wanting to reassure her, although his heart had started beating double time within his chest.

He told her swiftly in a sure voice, "No. I don't think that will be necessary. Has there ever been an inability to conceive in your family that you're aware of?" Peta's question had completely taken him by surprise. He hadn't given any thought to her not being able to conceive his child. Under the circumstances, he supposed that sole fact should have taken superiority over any other, but he found himself pushing the errant thought to the back of his mind as he looked down at her.

He hadn't found her to lose her. He decided in that instant that he was willing to take the chance on her being able to conceive his child. Anything else didn't bear thinking about. If any tests they took proved to be negative, Beale knew with a heartfelt certainty that Peta would refuse to marry him, and that was something he wasn't about to let happen. She already meant too much to him.

"Not that I know of." Her voice sounded a lot calmer, as if having gotten the encumberant thought off her chest, she could now move on.

"I was fully insured, but I have no idea of how long it will take to process all the paperwork. It might take months. I'll put everything into the hands of my solicitor, he'll know what to do," Peta told Beale later that morning as they were driving into Rockhampton. She added, "If I give him power-of-attorney, he can do all the running around. That will leave me free to go with you after we're married."

"Is there anyone else you'll need to contact, to tell them about our marriage?" He was still wondering about the man on the other end of that phone call.

"Some people down south, in Brisbane, but other than that there is nobody," she answered as she glanced idly at the passing scenery.

"How will they take the news, I wonder?" He couldn't help himself; he had to do some digging into her past, into her personal life.

"Now who's asking twenty questions?" Peta asked, trying to keep her voice as bland as possible.

Beale sent her a lop-sided grin, which tugged tenderly at her heartstrings. She wanted to reach out and touch him, but couldn't quite work up the courage to do so. Soon, she told herself, soon I'll feel comfortable doing those intimate little things like touching him. She fervently hoped that when that time came, Beale wouldn't shy away from her touch.

"I'm only trying to find out about the woman I'm about to marry," he told her pleasantly, "I already know that as far as family goes, you're all alone in the world, but you might have a girlfriend, or someone you share your news with. I've never met a woman yet who didn't like to share most things with a close friend."

"Or someone," she told him simply, "but there's no one here in town. Most of my friends live in Brisbane. I guess I'll have to make some phone calls sometime soon. Apart from anything else, they'll have to know about the fire."

Peta thought instantly of Nelson. He was probably her best friend and confidant. How she wished she could share the happenings of the last two days with him. She could imagine the stunned expression on his face when he heard of her upcoming marriage. He'd be horrified when she told him of the details concerning her agreement with Beale. That is, if she decided to tell him.

The trouble with Nelson was that he saw everything so clearly. There was no perhaps with Nelson. There was yes and then there was no, and he always knew which way to go without exception. To those people who didn't know him very well, his personality could almost be said to border on arrogance that was liberally laced with a touch of insolence. His only saving grace was that he possessed a heart of pure gold. There weren't enough adjectives in the English language to explain the person Nelson was, but Peta knew without a doubt that he'd be at her side in an instant if she needed him.

His ostentatious personality had pulled her out of the doldrums many times since the death of her grandmother. He had made it his business to keep a brotherly eye on her, calling in to see her whenever he was able, making sure that she was managing on her own. So why, she wondered, was she so reluctant to tell him about her forthcoming marriage to Beale? Marriages have been planned for less obscure reasons than this one and they have survived the test of time so I don't see why this one should fail. If we both try, who knows what could happen, she told herself simply, forcing down the lump which was trying to lodge itself in her throat.

Beale watched as the myriad of emotions played over her face. He still wasn't any closer to knowing if there was an ex-lover who had to be dealt with hovering somewhere in her background. Obviously, she wasn't going to divulge any information of that sort to him.

"Is that your way of telling me to mind my own business," he joked, having to concentrate on a series of bends in the road before he continued in a more serious voice, "Is there anyone you'd like to have with you when we marry, Peta?"

Peta was surprised by the fine mist of tears which covered her eyes as she thought of Nelson missing her wedding. She was sure the two men would like each other, and if there was one person she would like to be with her, it would be Nelson.

"There really isn't anyone close to me at the moment except for one person and he can't always be reached. He spends a lot of time on the road, but I'm sure I'll have his blessing when he finds out." She managed a weak smile, aware that he'd noticed the tears which she'd been trying unsuccessfully to hide.

Beale waited for a name, but when none was forthcoming, he was determined that he wasn't going to ask. Asking would mean that he cared and could possibly point to a feeling of jealousy which was totally out of the question. He wasn't jealous. He'd just been making polite conversation, trying to find out a few facts about the woman he was going to tie himself to for the rest of his life. Damn it all, she was going to be the mother of his children! He had a right to know about her background. Still, he told himself, those tears had been shed for someone that she felt very close to.

They had shared an enjoyable lunch at a little restaurant close to Peta's shop. Beale had told her a little about his family background. She already knew that he was the fifth generation to work Blackrock Downs. Since taking over the running of the station, he had introduced some very innovative, ground-breaking ideas into the everyday running of the station that had paid off handsomely.

Peta learnt that the station was situated close to the Queensland/Northern Territory border, just south of the Tropic of Capricorn. Try as she might, she couldn't comprehend the size of the place when Beale told her it covered an area of eighteen thousand square kilometres.

"But how do you look after such a vast area?" she had wanted to know, staring at him in astonishment. "Surely you'd need a small army to help you maintain it?"

"No, not really," he had smiled across at her. "I have twenty men on the payroll at the moment. Between us, we get the job done. Modern technology has made it a lot easier. We use a helicopter for a lot of the mustering, and we have a small plane that . . . ,"

"You have a helicopter?" Peta stated, looking at him in wide-eyed awe.

"Yes." He smiled, amused by her outburst. Then he raised his wineglass to her in a salute, saying softly, "To us."

Peta followed suite, and raising her glass she answered him shyly, "To us."

Opting to walk the short distance to her shop, Peta was appalled to see, in daylight, the amount of damage the fire had created. The entire building would have to be demolished. She instinctively took a step closer to Beale, who stood beside her.

"Oh dear," Peta said, as she surveyed the damage from the fire. She wasn't able to stop the wobble which caught at the roots of her voice as she walked through the burnt-out shell which until a few days ago had made up the major part of her life. "There really is nothing left, is there?" Unbidden, tears came to her eyes, and she wiped them away, trying to fight them back, not wanting to cry.

Beale, seeing the battle she was waging against the tears, put a comforting arm around her shoulders, drawing her close to his side. "Sometimes, even in the worst cases, things of value have been found at a later date."

She knew he was being optimistic, and was trying to lift her flagging spirits, so she told him in a voice which was more like her own, "Sometimes, but not always. I guess there's not much more I can do here, is there?"

Just as she was turning to leave, a glint of light caught her eye and she made her way towards the shiny object which was almost totally embedded in the rubble. She smiled as she bent down to retrieve the small tin, already knowing its contents. The tin was tarnished and blackened from the flames, but other than that, it was intact.

"Beale," she called his attention to the small object she held in her hand, "Look at what I found." She eased the top from the container, revealing to him the small gold cross which he had given her as a parting gift when she had dropped him at the service station.

"Well, I'll be darned!" he beamed down at her. "What would be the chances of finding that," He reached into the blackened tin, taking out the small cross and placed it in the palm of his hand. He continued, "So you wore it then? I wondered if you would. I thought perhaps you might throw it away."

Peta searched his face, wanting to know if he was being serious. "Why would I throw it away? I thought it was lovely. I put it on as soon as I opened the case. I had to take it off because the clasp broke while I was in the shop. I didn't want to risk losing it, so I put it in the tin under the counter. I especially loved the inscription, but I don't suppose you remember the words which were written in the actual case."

"Actually, I don't," he told her honestly, "but I'm still glad you liked it enough to wear it."

Peta smiled, knowing that she didn't really mind that he couldn't remember the inscription.

Chapter Four

"I feel as if I've known you forever. I realise how ridiculous that must sound, but it's true. When I think of how scared I was of you when I agreed to give you a lift ... it seems so long ago now instead of just a couple of weeks." Peta's thoughts returned to the night she'd first met Beale.

"Mmm, we do seem to be hitting it off rather well. I remember that night, too. I was starting to think you were going to drive off and leave me stranded on the side of the road." He smiled at the memory, chuckling to himself as he continued, "I didn't know what to do. It was obvious that you were afraid of me, so I decided the best thing I could do to put your mind at ease was to pretend to be asleep . . . ,"

"You were pretending to be asleep!" Peta wailed, horrified that he'd gone to such lengths to mollify her fears, "I'm sorry."

"That's okay. Now what was I saying . . . oh yes," he said, thoroughly enjoying the situation he had placed her in, "You looked so scared of me, every time I moved you'd tremble so I decided to put your mind at ease in the only way I could think of. I thought that if you thought I was asleep you'd start to relax."

"Was I really that transparent?" Peta asked, casting her mind back to that fateful day when Beale had walked into her life.

"Yes, I'm afraid you were, painfully so," he said, grinning down at her from his lofty height.

"Well, it won't ever happen again," she acknowledged smugly as she rose from the dinner table, intent on doing the dishes from their evening meal. She tacked on as an afterthought, saying the words before she'd thought them through, "Who knows, maybe one day we'll even love each other."

"It wouldn't hurt, that's for sure," he agreed as he took the tea towel from her and put it back on the rack. "Leave these for later. I'll make us some coffee. Go and sit on the verandah. I won't be long."

Peta looked across at him uncertainly. She couldn't fathom the implied meaning of his remark, and she found she was reluctant to ask. She wasn't sure she would like the answer he would give her. She could have kicked herself for saying that someday they might fall in love. This was supposed to be a business relationship they were entering into. Feelings of love were definitely not allowed, so why did she find herself so often lately thinking about love and Beale in the same instance.

She wasn't sure she liked the answer her mind was conjuring up for her. She couldn't love him. To love him would only bring hurt and suffering, because he didn't return those feelings. It would be better to forget about love entirely. It was the only chance of survival she had, but her heart told her it was already too late. Peta realised that she'd fallen in love with Beale.

In any other circumstances, to love the man you were going to marry would fill a girl with expectant happiness, but Peta was going to have to spend the rest of her life denying love's existence.

"Peta," Beale had been watching the conflicting emotions flit steadily across her face and he almost hated himself for asking her to marry him. How he wished he had the courage to tell her of his true feelings for her, but he didn't want to scare her away with their intensity. He hoped with all of his heart that the time would come when he could tell her he loved her, but until then he would have to continue with this ludicrous charade which he'd built around himself. He was finding it increasingly difficult to stop himself from touching her whenever they kissed. Consequently, he had all but stopped this very pleasant interlude by telling himself it was all for the best. But his body ached for her almost constantly.

Peta was looking up at him thoughtfully, almost expectantly, before he realised he'd been going to say something to her. What had he been going to say? His mind had been drained of all conscious thought. He shook his head slowly as he tried to think of some comforting words which would pull him through this emotional spiral which was trying to pull him down.

"Beale," Peta asked questioningly, as she waited for him to speak. She knew now with all certainty that she had made a grave mistake in speaking about love. He didn't love her. He was embarrassed, and now he didn't know how to answer her. When would she learn to keep her big mouth shut!

"It will be alright," he said at last, hoping his words would help to ease the anxiety she was feeling.

"Yes," she told him quietly, before adding, "If you don't mind, I won't have any coffee. I'm feeling rather tired after the day we've put in, so I might go to bed."

Beale watched her go through troubled eyes. He thought for a moment of calling her back and confessing his love for her, but he forced himself to hesitate, knowing this break was probably a good thing for both of them. He knew he certainly needed time to think.

Peta realised she'd slept in when looking at her bedside clock through bleary sleep-deprived eyes, she saw it was mid-morning. Beale usually knocked lightly on her door every morning telling her her coffee was ready and waiting, but obviously this morning he'd had better things to do with his time, although to be fair to him Peta thought, he could have tried to wake her up, found her still sleeping and had decided to let her rest.

The house was ominously silent, making Peta wonder if Beale was even home. A quick wander through to the front verandah revealed her suspicions were correct. Beale's car was missing from its usual parking spot under the cool branches of the tall gum tree at the side of the house.

Returning to the kitchen, she saw that last night's dishes had been done and put away. The room was spotless. There was an upturned coffee cup sitting on the sink, which was the only evidence that Beale had been here. So he didn't try to wake me, she thought dejectedly, or my cup would be here too.

She took a leisurely bath and try to soak away the gloomy feelings which were trying to overtake her concerning her relationship with Beale.

I guess a lot of things in my life will change from now on, she thought as she lowered herself into the tub, loving the feel of the soft bubbles as they caressed her skin. We haven't really discussed station life, so I don't really know what I'm in for. Just how does a station owner's wife behave, she wondered idly as she contemplated her toes as they protruded through the soft soapy suds? It wasn't as if she could produce a wifely manual which would give her a step-by-step description of how she should act once they arrived as man and wife. Man and wife . . . her senses heightened at the implication of her thoughts. There was really no turning back now. She had passed the point of no return, but she knew deep within her heart that she didn't want to return to the lonely life she'd been living.

It wasn't until she was back in the kitchen making herself a much needed cup of coffee that Peta spied the note that Beale had left for her. He had decided to go to the cattle sales at Gracemere. The note was short, using an economy of words, making Peta wonder at the frame of mind Beale had been in when he had scribed the information to her. Did he feel like he needed some breathing space away from her where he could think through his immediate actions of the last few days? Perhaps he only wanted to be in familiar surroundings, to be near people who usually lived and breathed the same atmosphere as he did himself.

Peta deduced that whatever the reason, she'd take advantage of his absence, for regardless of their reason for marrying she had decided she wanted her wedding day to be a day of special significance and remembrance. She wanted memories she could one day, in the far distant future, pass on to her children. She'd be damned if she was going to walk down the aisle in some drab outfit that wasn't worthy of the day that held a special place in every girl's heart. It might mean choosing a ready-made dress off the rack, but that was better than the alternative.

Suddenly Peta's mind whirled as she recalled seeing a dress that would perfectly fit the occasion. She remembered thinking how beautiful the gown was and how it would make a wonderful wedding dress for some lucky girl. With this thought in mind, Peta drove herself into Rockhampton. Her flagging spirits of the night before were instantly forgotten as she anticipated shopping for her forthcoming wedding day.

Beale and Peta hadn't discussed exactly when they would marry, or how their wedding day would proceed, so Peta hoped he wouldn't have any reservations about the plans she was thinking of making for both of them in his absence.

"Would you mind if I invited some associates to the wedding?" Beale asked her hesitantly.

Peta smiled across the table at him. "Of course not. Actually, I was going to ask you the same thing."

Beale raised an inquiring eyebrow to her as he waited for her to continue. She plunged into a one-sided conversation, telling him about her day, noting thankfully that he smiled openly as he listened intently to the tentative plans she'd made in his absence.

"You weren't joking when you said you've been busy, were you?" he told her once she'd finished speaking.

"Are you sure you don't mind? I thought perhaps I should wait and talk to you first. After all, it's your wedding day too." She bit her bottom lip as the thought of him as her husband filled her mind, permeating deliciously throughout her body, filling her with a conscious ache for him.

"No, I don't mind. Actually, I'm relieved that you're willing to take on the job. I wouldn't have known where to start," Beale told her truthfully, then tacked on in a more businesslike manner, "Since I'm staying in town a while longer, there are some station matters that I can attend to in person. Usually I have an agent who looks after this side of the business, but as long as I'm here I can do it personally. It helps sometimes when people can see first hand who they are dealing with, don't you think?"

Peta nodded her agreement. She had liked to take the personal approach herself when dealing with potential buyers. Then her mind was consumed once more with the preparations for their forthcoming wedding.

"There's still the actual date to fix. We have a couple of days to choose from," she told him, handing him the slip of paper the minister had given her, wanting him to choose the day when they would wed.

Beale took a moment to skim over the dates. He couldn't see any reason to procrastinate. "How about the fifteenth? Does that give you enough time to get ready?"

Peta's heart leapt within her chest. Five days. In five days, she would walk down the aisle to start a new life with Beale. She purposely veered her mind away from all the things this marriage would lack, like love, but she told herself resolutely she had known from the start that love would be a stranger in their relationship. It was to be a marriage of convenience, but it wasn't going to be in name only. Beale needed an heir if he was going to keep his family home intact, and he was marrying her as a means to that end. She would be wise to remember that. In time, he might grow to love her. Stranger things had happened. They had become friends, so who was to say that they couldn't become lovers in every term of the word.

"It should be enough time. Since we aren't having a reception, it's only a matter of getting the paperwork filled out, and that shouldn't take long. It's a good thing that we both have our birth certificates, otherwise we'd have to send away for them. That can take weeks," she told him before turning to the subject which had been nagging at her for most of the day, "Beale, what are we going to tell people? Everyone is sure to ask us how we met."

Today, while in town, she had run into one of her former customers who had wanted to know if she was going to relocate her shop. She hadn't known exactly how to answer the simple query, so she had simply told the woman that she was getting married, therefore she wouldn't be seeking to reopen her business.

Beale frowned at her. Clearly he hadn't given the matter very much consideration at all.

Peta continued, "Do you want your family and friends to know how we met? I'm not sure that I do. I really don't want to have people snickering at me behind my back," she bit her lip, the thought of people knowing their intimate details didn't bear thinking about, "Couldn't we fabricate some innocent story that would satisfy everyone's curiosity why we're getting married. I know it's not exactly the truth, but . . . ," her voice trailed off as she looked across at him, hoping she would see acceptance in the look he was directing at her.

"I suppose we could tell everyone that we've known each other for a year or so. I first started coming to Rockhampton regularly around that time. In fact, most of the people from Blackrock think I've been coming into town to see a woman, so as an explanation it wouldn't go astray, but what about you, do you have anyone who would want a detailed explanation of why you're going to suddenly be getting married?" Beale wanted to know. His mind returned to the phone call he had overheard the day he'd been in the shop, picking up his mother's parcel.

"No. No, not really." Her mind automatically shied away from Nelson, who would literally tear her to pieces when he found out what she was planning to do. She would contact him and tell him if she could, but that was one of the problems about his job, he could not be contacted unless he wanted to be contacted. She could have used his guidance and his wisdom these last few days, using him as a sounding board for all the doubts and fears that she'd been experiencing.

Beale had watched as Peta's face displayed the emotions of her thoughts. Clearly she had wanted to talk to someone other than himself. He wondered why she wasn't able to do so and then discarded the thought from his mind. She was going to marry him, not this other nameless, faceless person who wasn't even on the scene. Perhaps they'd quarrelled prior to ending their evening, but Beale wasn't going to tie himself up in knots worrying about a lot of maybes, so he told her, "Okay, that's settled then. We've been seeing each other for a year. This time around I asked you to marry me and you accepted. Yes?"

"Yes," Peta told him, and then asked, "Do you want your mother to come to the wedding?"

"Oh, I don't know. She might want to make the trip, but it seems an awfully long way to travel when she'll only have to turn around and go home again."

"Beale! That's an awful thing to say. If I was your mot . . . , what?" He was grinning at her.

"She's coming. I've already told her. I just have to let her know when and now that I have that important piece of information, I can pass it on. I can assure you she'll be here on the next plane to see the girl who has stolen her son's heart."

"Oh." Peta tried not to think of the words he had used. Stolen her son's heart. If only that was the case. How happy she would be. She added hastily, "I'll have to get a room ready for her."

"Hey, do I detect a note of fear at the prospect of meeting your future mother-in-law," Beale asked her, noting the heightened colour that ebbed and flowed on her cheeks.

Peta grabbed at this idea. Anything was better than having him think her flushed cheeks were due to the remark he had so innocently made about his heart.

"A bit," she lied, "but I'm sure we'll get along famously." If truth be told, Peta was looking forward to meeting Beale's mother. Being accepted by the people Beale lived and worked alongside would make the transition so much easier. They would be a closely knit community, having little to do with the outside world. Beale had told her they were extremely isolated, so it was important that they all got along with one another.

Beale was amused at Peta's nervousness as they waited in the airport terminal for his mother's flight to arrive.

"She's a very ordinary person really, very down to earth. She takes pleasure in the little things that life offers," he told her yet again in answer to Peta's query. He added, "You'll probably get on very well. From what I've been able to observe of you in the short time we've been together, you have similar tastes to her in a lot of things. Don't worry, everything will be fine. She's not an ogre, Peta, she's my mother."

That's easy for you to say, Peta thought to herself, not for the first time, for it seemed she was a trifle nervous about meeting his mother after all. Beale wasn't the one who was being uprooted out of a secure, safe environment, one where he'd been extremely content, to be taken to a place, god only knew where, plonked down and then be expected to carry on as if nothing earth shattering had happened. Her complete way of life was about to change, so he'd have to forgive her if she was just a little sceptical about the whole thing.

Peta voiced none of her misgivings, however, but merely stated, "I'm sure you're right, Beale, but still, as you say, she is your mother and I'm the woman you're about to marry," saying these words still tied Peta up in knots, "She wouldn't be normal if she wasn't just a little curious."

"Perhaps, but just remember, we're in this together. If you feel trapped or don't know what to say, I'm just a look away," he told her. He knew as soon as Peta met his mother, her fears would instantly dissolve. His mother had the ability to put people at their ease. He'd seen it happen many times during his life when time after time at home on the station his father would ruffle feathers with his forthright opinions and his mother would settle them down.

He was thankful that he had inherited the best from both of his parents. In the past, since taking over the running of the station, he'd had to wear a steel glove when tough decisions had to be made, but he prided himself on the fact that he was astute enough to know how to wield the authority that went with the wearing of that glove. It was this quality that made Beale the man he was.

Reaching out to her, he took Peta's hand in his and gently caressed her open palm. "It will all work out, Peta. I haven't found you to lose you."

Her heart leapt at these words, and although they weren't words of love exactly, they did smack of commitment and harmony.

Looking up into his face, Peta told him solemnly, "I'm sure you're right. I'm just nervous," then added in a lighter tone, "It's not every day that a girl goes through the ordeal of meeting her future mother-in-law, though, is it? Just be thankful you don't have to do it."

Beale smirked at her, raising his eyebrows in such a ludicrous manner that Peta was forced to laugh.

"Come on, up with you, that's Mum's flight they're announcing," he said as he pulled her gently to her feet bringing her into the circle of his arms as he did so, "Do you think anyone would notice if I kissed you?"

"Probably, but I don't think I care," Peta told him boldly. Her heart leapt at the unexpected intimacy which was flowing freely between them. She looked up into Beale's face and wished yet again that she had the strength to tell him how she felt. She detected a muscle jumping energetically along his strong jawline, which told her he wasn't totally immune to her brand of charm either. Before she thought through her actions, Peta reached up and gently caressed the erratic pulse point, loving the feel of his newly shaven skin beneath her soft fingers.

Covering her hand with his own, Beale removed her hand from his face. He gently, but firmly, placed both of her arms around his neck before putting his own arms around her trim waist and then drew her into a closer embrace. He brought his lips down slowly until they covered hers in a lingering kiss that left her slightly breathless.

Releasing her slowly, he rested his forehead against the top of her head. Peta could feel the slight tremble that was coursing throughout his body. It was offset by the trembling that was, at this moment, causing havoc within her own body.

Beale told her somewhat thickly, "I think we'll be alright, Peta. I know you enjoyed that kiss as much as I did. Who knows, love can follow if we're patient."

Peta knew she couldn't deny Beale's reasoning, but the only thing she would change in his statement was the fact that she loved him already, but she knew she would have to patiently play the waiting game to see if he came to love her. It was a gamble she was willing to take.

Nodding her agreement was the best response she could muster. Looking around her, she could see the curious glances they were being treated to. Some people were smiling openly. Some, she knew, would not be so charitable, but she found she didn't care. If Beale was to kiss her again, she would embrace him eagerly, and to hell with all the onlookers.

Peta's eyes were radiant when she finally met Beale's mother a few minutes later. Her happiness was evident for all to see.

Beale clasped her hand as he made the introductions. He gave his mother a warm hug before giving her a quick kiss on the cheek. "Mum, this is Peta. Jupiter to be exact, but for some reason that I can't fathom, she prefers Peta."

"Hello, Peta. It's wonderful to finally meet you. Beale has been so secretive about your identity until now that I was starting to think he was making you up." Peta's first impression of Beale's mother was one of beauty. She was tall and slim and carried herself with a natural elegance. Her hair, black like her son's, was peppered with gray, but far from detracting from her beauty, the onset of age added to her natural elegance.

"A guy gets to an age, Mum, when he doesn't have to tell his mother everything, you know," Beale told his mother throwing a wink in for good measure making Peta blush profusely as she remembered the kiss they'd just shared.

Oh bother, she thought hotly to herself, now she will think Beale and I have been intimate. She knew it was useless trying to explain the reason for the blush, especially when, as she looked up into Beale's amused face, he had a silly grin plastered over his face which practically told its own story. He squeezed her hand, which he had taken in a light grasp, and Peta realised he was trying to make this meeting between the two of them as painless for her as he could.

"Hello, Mrs. Jacobs," she said, taking her hand out of Beale's casual grasp and offered it instead to his mother. Smiling sweetly, she tacked on, "Don't take any notice of Beale. I'm sure that between the two of us we can make him toe the line."

"What's this? Ganging up on me already," Peta could see the lights dancing in his eyes as he looked down at her. So he hadn't minded her attempt at breaking the ice between his mother and herself.

Beale's mother ignored Peta's outstretched hand, telling her handshakes were for strangers. "Families greet each other with hugs where I come from. It's a tradition I'd like to see passed on if that's alright with you and, please, call me Nancy."

"It's more than alright," Peta agreed, stepping into the arms of her future mother-in-law, liking her instantly. She looked across at Beale, who threw her a knowing smile that smacked of 'I told you so.'

They took Beale's mother to lunch before heading back to the beach, and Peta was able to bring her up to date on the plans they had made so far concerning the wedding.

"This place has certainly grown since the last time I was here," Nancy told them as she looked around with interest, "Do you think we'll have time to do a bit of shopping, Peta, before you go out to the station. I'd love to look at some craft shops while I'm in town. It's always so much better shopping in person. Catalogues are excellent, but there's nothing like a hand's on approach when you're looking for that certain something."

Peta beamed across at her. "I'd love that. I just happen to know where you'll get some excellent bargains having run a craft shop myself."

"Wonderful. Beale, you won't mind if I steal Peta away from you for a while, will you?"

"So you two finally remembered that I'm here. No, I don't mind in the slightest. It will give me a chance to finish up the business I was telling you about." He was smiling as he delivered this bit of information. "Speak of the devil, there's Rob over there now. Will you two lovely ladies excuse me for a moment while I see if I can set up a meeting for tomorrow," Beale was up and out of his seat as he was speaking, intent on seeing the man who was sitting by himself on the other side of the restaurant.

His mother waved him off, telling him to take his time saying that it would give her a chance to talk to Peta about the wedding.

Peta told her about the plans they'd made, asking her if she could think of anything that she might have forgotten.

"No, you seem to have thought of everything. Trust Beale to spring a wedding on you out of the blue like this. His father did the same thing to me. It must run in his blood," she said simply then tacked on, "It's funny the things that draw you initially to a person, isn't it? Sometimes it can be something as simple as a look, a caress, a familiar smell . . . ," Peta thought she detected a wistful longing for the memories that had filtered into Nancy's mind about her dead husband.

"He must have been a wonderful man," she said quietly, not really knowing how to comfort the other woman.

"Yes, he was. Beale has a lot of his qualities. He's a good man," she stated matter-of-factually. Peta wondered if Nancy was imparting this piece of information to her, subtly telling her not to hurt her son.

But what about me, her heart cried? Who's here to tell him I'm a good person, that I'm worthy of his love should he ever decide to bestow some form of affection on me.

She simply answered, "Yes, I know."

She was treated to a shrewd smile as the other woman asked her, "You love him very much, don't you?'

She knows her heart cried out painfully. She knows. Now what do I do, Peta asked herself as she felt the panic rising up in her chest. What if Beale's mother inadvertently tells him about the admission she had just made, that she declared her undying love for him?

Peta didn't need to give the question a second thought and answered truthfully, "Yes, I do."

Peta's eyes misted over with tears, and she tenaciously tried to push them away with the palms of her hands. She felt she was letting Beale down with this show of weakness in front of his mother.

"I'm sorry," she murmured self-consciously when she had herself under control once more, "I don't know what came over me."

"Oh, my dear, it's perfectly natural. You're about to be married. It's unknown territory that you're about to venture into. Of course you're bound to be a little scared. Do you know I was so scared before my marriage to Beale's father that I almost ran away?"

"No, but why?" Peta wanted to know. She couldn't believe that this self-assured woman sitting directly across from her could ever be afraid of anyone or anything.

"True. Oh, I loved him, but he had a side to him I rarely saw while we were courting. There was a hardness about him, there has to be when you're running a cattle station, so many decisions to be made which ultimately affected the lives of so many people, but I knew he loved me and it was this thought that kept me at his side. We had a happy marriage for nearly forty years. He was thinking of handing the reins over to Beale when he was killed."

"I'm sorry." Peta reached across the table and patted Nancy's hand, "It must have been a terrible time for you."

"Yes, but life goes on. I've had the pleasure of watching Beale grow into the kind of a man his father was, but without the hardness," she smiled across at Peta as she told her, "for that fact you can thank me."

"Thank you," Peta answered, knowing that an answer hadn't really been necessary.

For the next half an hour she was regaled with stories about Beale's father and about Beale, himself. His father had been well liked and respected by all who knew him. Beale's mother then told her a little about her son. For this, Peta was truly thankful because it gave her an added insight into her future husband's life. When Beale had stepped into his father's shoes and taken over the everyday running of Blackrock Downs after his father's accidental death, he'd had the approval of an entire community. Over the years he had gained a reputation of being hard, like his father, but fair to everyone that he had dealings with. The only subject that his mother shied away from was Beale's former girlfriends. Peta longed to ask, but refrained from doing so. She wasn't sure that she'd appreciate knowing about his other conquests, especially coming from his mother who, she knew, would be biased towards her son.

"Miss Masters, hello, I was hoping you'd arrive while I was here. You must have a guardian angel sitting on your shoulder. Someone greeted Peta as soon as she stepped from the car.

They were on their way home when Peta had remembered that she had promised to call in to the police station while she was in town. Inspector Irving had called her, saying he wished to see her. She was told by a kindly police woman that the Inspector was at the site of the fire. He had been kindness itself on the night of the fire, but she had been too shocked to take in much of what he had said to her.

Now she answered in total amazement, "You've got to be kidding. How can you think that?" The man must be mad, she thought as she gazed at the chaos which surrounded her.

"Now, now, please hear me out," he insisted, holding up a gloved hand against Peta's tirade, "While I know you've lost most of your belongings, there is one small piece of good news for you to latch on to. It seems your neighbours, on the night of the fire, knowing that you lived at the back of the shop, broke your door down and were able to save a considerable amount of stock and also some personal items. They thought you were still inside, so they thought they were rescuing you."

Peta looked at him, too stunned to utter a sound. People had actually risked their lives trying to retrieve a few measly possessions for her! She felt a lump rising in her throat at the kindness of the people who had been her fellow tenants.

When she could finally speak, it was to voice a strangled, "You're joking!" The implication of the Inspector's words moved her beyond belief.

"Beale, did you hear that?" Peta called to him. He was looking through a growing pile of rubble that comprised tumbled walls and debris from the fire. He raised quizzical eyebrows as he covered the short distance to where she stood virtually rooted to the spot.

He could see that something had happened to upset her and instinctively put a harbouring arm around her slim shoulders, wanting to protect her.

"What is it?" he asked, looking from one to the other.

"My neighbours. My lovely, wonderful neighbours broke in on the night of the fire and saved some of my things. Can you believe that? They could have been killed! They were really trying to save me, but I wasn't here." Peta looked up into Beale's face, knowing she was babbling, but for the life of her she couldn't seem to stop herself.

"That's wonderful news, sweetheart," he told her as he gathered her into his arms.

Peta sobbed into his chest, not really knowing why it was happening. At this stage she didn't know what had been saved, but she was grateful to the people who had risked their own lives believing that she was trapped inside the burning building.

Beale held her securely while she cried, whispering to her, telling her to let it all go, that he was there for her. He stroked her hair as the soft, silky strands rested beneath his hand. He loved the feel of the luxurious softness as her long tresses came into contact with his calloused palms. He bestowed soft kisses into the silky strands, breathing deeply, taking the now familiar scent of her into his nostrils.

Peta moved reluctantly away from Beale's comforting embrace. She had felt secure while she was being held within the steely strength of his casual embrace. She looked up into his face, giving him a slightly wobbly smile of gratitude. She knew she must look a fright with her tear-stained face, and vivid images of Beale's blond friend came unbidden into her mind to haunt her. Peta was sure the other woman wouldn't spoil her perfect image by doing something so mundane as crying. Lately, crying seemed to be second nature to Peta.

"I'm sorry," she mumbled against his chest before lifting her tear-stained eyes to him. "I always seem to be crying lately. I'm not normally so emotional."

"Apology accepted. It's not every day your business is gutted by fire either. It's been quite a day all round, hasn't it?" he said as he returned her watery smile with a brilliant one of his own. His emerald gaze gave her the encouragement she needed to press on.

She cast him another watery smile before telling him simply, "Beale, I'd like to arrange a meeting with the other tenants. I want to thank them for their kindness, and for trying to save my things, and of course, me. Can you imagine it, trying to fight your way into a burning building? Dear god, they could have been killed." She shuddered and Beale held her closer, wanting to shield her from the pain she was feeling.

"That sounds like a good idea, but how will you be able to contact them?"

"Surely Inspector Irving must have a forwarding address for everyone?" With this decision made, Peta felt a lot better. It had been troubling her that she hadn't seen any of the other tenants since the fire, but under the circumstances she guessed that was to be expected. Although she hadn't gotten to know them as neighbours, they had all suffered the same fate and as far as she was concerned, that was the bond that held them together. Perhaps she could invite them to the wedding. She would ask Beale later, but she was sure that he wouldn't mind.

The only dark cloud on an almost perfect horizon had occurred on the night of Beale's mother's arrival.

They had decided that they wouldn't have a traditional reception, opting instead to go out to dinner after the ceremony, which was to be at five o'clock in the afternoon. Beale had left these arrangements entirely up to Peta, telling her he trusted her judgement completely. He had invited some colleagues to the wedding, telling Peta he'd run into them on his visits to the sale yards. One of them had consented to be his best man and would meet Beale at the church.

Peta had arranged for one of her former customers, Sherry, to be her matron of honour, as she was someone who Peta had formed a friendship of sorts with. The girl had been thrilled to be asked and had accepted immediately.

Peta was therefore dismayed when Sherry's husband phoned to tell her that his wife had been in an accident and was in hospital. He passed on his regrets, telling her that his wife was very sorry. He had laughingly told her she had wanted to walk down the aisle on crutches just so the wedding wouldn't be spoiled by her unfortunate bad luck, but the doctor had vetoed this idea.

"Oh dear," Peta wailed when she put the phone back on its receiver, "What am I going to do now?"

Who could she ask this late in the proceedings? The wedding was only two days away, making her realise just how alone she was. She had severed most of the ties she had with her friends down south when she had opted to move to Rockhampton to start her business. It saddened her to think there was no one close to her to whom she could turn to help her celebrate her wedding day to Beale.

She briefly gave some thought to asking another of her former customers to join the wedding party, but she decided at the last minute to not do this. Her wedding day was starting to turn into a fiasco and one of her own making at that, but she had so wanted to be married in a church, to have her vows solemnised and ordained by a man of the cloth.

When she explained the situation tearfully to Beale a few minutes later, he couldn't see the problem. He looked thoughtfully at her for a minute before asking, "So it doesn't really matter who you have up there with you, as long as you have someone. Am I correct in making that assumption?"

Peta mumbled something that he couldn't really understand because of her heightened emotional state, but he took it to be a yes.

"Okay then, no problem," Peta lifted tear-stained eyes to miserably look at him. "We'll ask my mother. I'm sure she'd consider it an honour to be our matron of honour."

He pulled a hanky out of his shirt pocket and dabbed delicately at the tears which were trickling slowly down her pale cheeks. "I've started carrying spares," he told her lightly, trying to get her to smile. He was rewarded when he saw the ghost of a smile flit across her pouting mouth.

"Well." he asked when an answer wasn't forthcoming, "What do you say?"

"That would be lovely," Peta sniffed as she tried to pull herself together. She had certainly been on an emotional roller coaster lately. It was a side of her personality that she didn't know she possessed. "Do you think she'll agree?"

"We can only ask. Come on, there's no time like the present." Beale pulled her to her feet, drawing her into his arms, where he held her securely for a few minutes. Peta made no attempt to move or to mask the pleasure being held by him gave her. She was finding it increasingly difficult to remain passive in his arms. Letting her go, he planted a quick kiss on her parted lips. "That's for luck," he told her, "but we won't need it."

Peta wondered what Beale would say if she was to tell him she loved him with every fibre of her being. She smiled a sad little smile when she thought how Victorian her thoughts were, but that was how strongly she felt. Would such an outburst embarrass him when he didn't return her love in such an all-consuming way? The words were burning on her lips and she longed to utter them, to blurt them out with a devil may care longing, but she was afraid to do so, instead she silently told him in her heart. I love you, Beale, oh so very much.

Nancy was overjoyed to be asked and accepted immediately, but she told Peta worriedly, "I don't have anything suitable to wear. I have a dress for the wedding and even though it's beautiful, it won't be suitable. What was your friend going to wear, perhaps . . ."

She got no further, for Beale's hoot of laughter drowned out whatever she had been going to say. "Isn't that just like a woman saying she has nothing to wear," Now he'd heard it all and from his mother to boot.

He was treated to a cold stare and told that if he couldn't behave himself, he could leave the room.

"We hired a dress for her." Peta felt foolish. Because of her stubborn push for a church wedding, she was being inundated with these stupid problems. If she was to relent and had a civil ceremony, most of her problems would magically disappear. Then it wouldn't matter who she had with her. As it was, she didn't have anyone to give her away and would walk down the aisle by herself. It just wouldn't matter one tiny bit.

She glanced helplessly from Beale to his mother and then back to Beale. Both of them were looking at her, waiting patiently for her to continue. Suddenly the burden seemed too much for Peta's slim shoulders to carry. She felt she was suffocating and needed to get away, to breathe in some fresh air away from all of these trite problems.

Mumbling a hurried, "Excuse me," Peta pushed herself away from the table and fled down the hallway towards the front door and away to freedom into the welcoming darkness which obligingly swallowed her up in its beckoning shadows.

Beale would have followed her, but his mother astutely called him back, explaining Peta's need for solitude.

Peta wasn't sure how long she sat looking out at the surf. Time seemed to be irrelevant at the moment and of little consequence. She needed to be alone with her thoughts, and she fervently hoped that Beale and his mother would recognise her need to put her life into its proper perspective by herself.

The sound of the waves gently lapping against the shore soothed her jangled nerves, creating a buffer between herself and the real world. Her eyes had become accustomed to the silvery light as it filtered down through the trees that grew in abundance near the shoreline. The moon appeared like a huge, bright ball hanging low in the sky. Its only accompaniment was millions of stars shining out of a perfect night sky with not a cloud in sight to mar their brilliance. She was being treated to a spectacular show of nature, but she was too miserable to take in the beauty that was before her. She would give it all up if Beale would only love her, if indeed he had any feelings for her at all other than needing to marry her in order to produce an heir for him, allowing him to keep his property. It was in his best interests to keep her happy.

Peta caught her breath when she witnessed a shooting star falling to its doom, for she knew it was on a clear-cut path to headlong destruction with the earth's atmosphere, but it looked spectacular as she watched the fiery tail fizzle out into nothingness.

She hoped her flight into marriage wouldn't suffer the same plight. She recalled a rhyme she had often recited as a child and wished on the falling star, wishing that Beale loved her.

Beale, her heart cried out sadly. Peta smiled suddenly in the darkness, knowing this children's rhyme wouldn't bring her heart's desire to fruition. One didn't make wishes on falling stars and who in their right mind would pin their hopes and dreams on such a thing. People called Jupiter Masters, she cried out silently into the night. She recalled her grandmother telling her that wishes were three a penny, but dreams were covered in gold.

How she wished her grandmother was here to share this time with her. She badly needed her guidance and her wisdom to see her through the next few very important days.

She thought of her wedding dress, safely packed away in folds of tissue paper to keep it free of creases. She had been so lucky to find it. It saddened her to think of her good luck stemming from the broken dreams of another. Her dress would never be worn by the person for whom it had been originally made. She had been told that at the last minute the girl had cancelled her wedding plans and gone overseas. Peta had bought it for a song because of the circumstances. Loving the dress on sight, she had scooped it up, knowing it was perfect for her. The dress could have been designed with her in mind. The delicate lace and embroidered pearl trim was exactly what Peta would have chosen for herself.

Sighing audibly, Peta knew she had to go back and present Beale with an explanation for her hurried departure. It hadn't been her intention to hurt either of them, and she fervently hoped that they realised this. Possibly she was suffering from pre-wedding day jitters. She knew she wouldn't be the first bride to suffer an attack of this kind.

When she finally built up the courage to go back inside, she apologised to both Beale and his mother, telling Nancy that she would be delighted if she would be her matron of honour. "I know that, dear," the other woman told her warmly, "We knew you needed some time to yourself to sort things out. Now if you don't mind, I think I'll go to bed. I'm going to need my beauty sleep if I'm going to be part of the wedding party."

Finding herself alone with Beale after his mother's departure wasn't easy at first. She could think of nothing to say to him, and he didn't seem inclined to add his thoughts to the conversation, either.

Finally he said to her in a voice that was very low and throbbed with emotion, "Do you want to call this wedding off, Peta, because if you do I won't force you into a union that you find unpleasant?"

Had she heard him correctly? Was he giving her the option to walk away, or was he telling her to walk away? Either way, Peta didn't want to go, couldn't he see that for himself? Taking her courage in both hands, she asked him quietly, "Is that what you want, Beale, for me to walk away?" Her heart was in her throat as she waited for his answer.

"Hell, no!" he exclaimed. "That's not what I want. Anything but that. I want us to get married, Peta, but I need to know that you want it too."

Heaving a great sigh of relief, Peta felt as if a weight had been magically lifted from her shoulders. "I do," she told him simply.

She was incredibly busy taking care of all the last-minute details that seemed to have been added to her already overcrowded agenda. She spent a wonderful day shopping with Beale's mother. Nancy had been a tower of strength guiding her through the emotional minefield, taking her forever forward through the highs and lows towards her wedding day. Peta found herself wondering, not for the first time, if this emotional turmoil struck other brides on the eve of their wedding day.

Peta was amazed at how quickly the days flew by. It was almost as if Father Time wanted to hasten her date with destiny, for all too soon she woke up on the day of her wedding. It amazed her how calm she felt when for the last few days she'd been constantly bordering on the verge of hysteria and tears.

Last night, she'd opted to move back into town prior to the wedding and was staying at a motel close to the church where she and Beale would be wed. Defending her actions, she'd told him it was bad luck for the bride and groom to see each other before their wedding.

"Hogwash, " Beale exclaimed to this piece of traditional hype, but if it made Peta happy he'd go along with it, but only for a night.

"Anyway, I'm sure your mother will enjoy having you to herself for a few hours, at least. It's only for a day, Beale," she told him, smiling up into his unhappy face.

"How am I supposed to transform myself into a blushing bride without outside help," she had asked him, secretly revelling because he didn't want her to go.

"You look fine to me. In fact, I think you're beautiful just the way you are." He had gathered her up into his arms then and kissed her passionately, ending any conversation between them.

Peta's heart had leapt at the contact between them, as it always did. Surely this was a good sign that their marriage was going to work.

Lying in bed, she recalled the conversation she'd shared with Beale last night. She stretched luxuriously as she remembered their kisses and felt her body go hot with wanting him. She had been telling him that after their marriage he'd be stuck with her for better or worse.

His answer was to smile and reach for her again, but Peta had been adamant about wanting to know if he'd discussed the subject of their marriage with his mother.

Sighing audibly, Beale retreated to his side of the car. A fact that had made Peta laugh. It wasn't that she hadn't wanted his kisses, but she had also wanted to know how his mother felt about her.

"Mum likes you. She keeps asking me why I kept you a secret for so long."

"Do you think she suspects anything?" Peta had wanted to know. They had told Beale's mother they were marrying because they loved each other and that the destruction of her shop had hastened their decision to marry.

Beale had certainly been more attentive since his mother's arrival. His explanation to Peta had been that they had to look the part of expectant lovers if his mother was to believe in their marriage. Peta had cherished every look, every touch that Beale gave her, resolutely pushing to the back of her mind the knowledge that he was only playing a part.

"I don't know. She knows about the will, but I'm afraid she'll keep her own counsel on the subject of our marriage. The one thing I can promise you is that she would never malign you to another living soul. She doesn't have a malicious bone in her body."

"I kind of figured that out for myself. I think she's lovely. I'm sure we'll get along famously," she told him warmly, then tacked on for the heck of it, "Your mother is perfect mother-in-law material."

He had laughed then. A deep throaty laugh that had Peta's nerve ends jangling with suppressed emotion. She could see the amusement shining out of his beautiful emerald eyes as he gazed across the short distance towards her.

"Will we be alright, Beale?" she had asked him suddenly, instantly wiping the laughter from his eyes.

"I think so," he answered her softly, "especially when you respond to me so energetically and with so much enthusiasm. In a few years, we'll have forgotten the circumstances under which we met. By then we'll just be the happily married couple living out in the backblocks."

Peta smiled, wishing with all of her heart that his prophecy regarding their future life together would come true.

"Beale, I . . . ," Peta had nearly blurted out that she loved him. She was feeling so emotional at the moment that she couldn't trust herself in his presence.

"What?" Beale wanted to know as he gazed steadily across at her. She'd been going to say something important, he was sure of it, but now her face was a closed book. One he wasn't able to interpret.

"Nothing. It's getting late. If you don't mind, I think I'll go in now. Tomorrow's going to be a big day for both of us." Upon saying this she virtually fled from the car, leaving him staring after her with a puzzled look on his handsome face.

Chapter Five

"I NOW PRONOUNCE YOU man and wife," the minister's simple words slowly permeated into Peta's mind. Beale's wife. She was now Beale's wife . . . for better or worse. From this moment on there was to be no turning back on the vows that they had just made to each other in the presence of God and the small gathering of people who had been invited to witness their pledge to love each other.

The minister was looking at her fondly, smiling his obvious approval of the marriage of these two young people. To Beale he said in a fatherly voice, "You may kiss your bride now, Mr. Jacobs."

Peta felt slightly embarrassed and unsure of what she should do. She turned bewildered eyes towards this stranger who had just become her husband.

As Beale looked steadily down at her, she thought his eyes were the most incredible green she had ever seen. The soft evening light had picked up the emerald highlights and had thrown them into a vibrant, shining colour.

He smiled briefly, noticing the uncertainty that had sprung into her lovely gold-flecked eyes. How he wished he could tell her she was the treasure he'd been looking for all of his life.

They were lightly holding hands. Peta could feel her body traitorously trembling and hoped that Beale wouldn't notice and think she was afraid. Taking a deep breath to compose herself, Peta stepped forward, bringing her body into intimate contact with his. Although their bodies barely touched, she felt strengthened by his closeness. It will be alright, she told herself as she raised her lips to his, letting him know with this small gesture his kiss would be welcomed.

He touched his lips lightly to Peta's intending for the kiss to be brief, but as always, when he kissed her, all rational thought of letting her go was forgotten and he gathered her up into his arms as their kiss deepened. It was only the hoots of laughter and the clapping that could be heard emanating from the pews in the back of the church that made him reluctantly release her.

"Hold off, Beale," his friend told him good-naturedly, slapping him on the shoulder, "You're not alone yet!"

Beale had the grace to look shamefaced as he gazed down into Peta's upturned face. Her cheeks were flowing with colour, and he thought she had never looked more beautiful.

"You look beautiful," he told her softly on an impulse, knowing he'd cherish the memory of the way she looked today for as long as he lived.

"That's the way, mate," his friend told him, "you're getting the hang of it. Just tell her that every so often and you'll be jake."

Beale looked down at Peta. His look told her he was sorry for the remarks of his uncouth colleagues. He shook his head slightly, trying to rid himself of the image his mind was conjuring up of her resting in his arms, but he knew she would always occupy a place there for all time. A small smile played around his lips. He gently took her hand in his as he prepared to follow the minister into a small alcove at the side of the church where they were to sign the register.

The minister had kindly consented to Peta changing out of her wedding dress in his house, which was situated a short distance behind the church. They had farewelled most of their guests and had put up with a lot of good-natured bantering from people they both knew who had wanted to wish them every happiness, but Peta was definitely relieved when she could, at last, make her escape to the relative safety of the small bedroom where her clothes had been laid out waiting for her.

She was acutely conscious of the unaccustomed weight of the thick diamond studded wedding ring which felt unnaturally heavy on her finger, and she twisted it nervously as she gazed out of the window. She couldn't see the church from where she stood, but she was treated instead to a beautiful view of a garden full of fragrant flowers. Their combined fragrance wafted through the open window, and Peta breathed in the heady perfume, loving the exhilarating feeling the flowers produced in her.

She was reminded of her grandmother's garden which had always been ablaze with riotous colours from the various blooms she would plant. Her grandmother had been an avid gardener in her youth and when she could no longer do the physical work that was required to keep her garden looking like the show piece it was, she would sit in her comfortable chair under the shade of an enormous gum tree and direct Peta to do the work for her.

This was a job that Peta had loved. Her love of all growing things was just one more thing that she'd had in common with her grandmother. She wondered if she'd be able to have a garden in her new home or would the harsh Australian sun destroy all of her efforts to establish herself in her new environment. She must remember to ask Beale.

"This won't do," she told herself, dragging her mind back to the present and the task that lay before her.

She started to divest herself of the lovely white gown, marvelling yet again at how lucky she had been to find such a beautiful creation at such short notice. She had already decided that she would use the material from the dress to make a christening gown for their first child. There was more than enough for a whole layette, she thought as she put the dress back into its layers of tissue paper. To leave it like this would be a waste, for she knew the fabric would probably yellow in time. She had thought for a time of taking it back to the shop where she had bought it, but she couldn't bear the thought of her lovely dress being passed on from bride to bride, or possibly hanging forlornly in the shop never to be worn again.

For her going-away outfit, Peta had chosen a lovely eggshell blue silk dress and like her wedding dress, she had loved it at first sight. She wasn't known for keeping abreast of fashion and had spied this particular dress in an opportunity shop of all places when she'd been shopping with Nancy. Both women had marvelled over its superior quality. It looked to be almost brand new, however Peta had voiced her concerns to Nancy about wearing a second-hand garment.

"Nonsense," the other woman told her, "It's perfect for you. You look absolutely beautiful." She guided Peta over to the full-length mirror and positioned her in front of it so that she could see her reflection.

"See what I mean?" she had told her simply.

Peta studied the image of the woman who stood looking back at her. At the moment, she was biting her lower lip indecisively, but she was forced to admit that the dress did look lovely. The soft fabric clung suggestively to her soft curves, showing off her full rounded hips. The skirt fell just below her knees, flouncing out from her hips ever so slightly with just the softest suggestion of a flare. She raised her eyes to the soft bodice, loving the way the dress had been fashioned. The neckline was low and slightly cowled, forming layers of soft fabric across the front of Peta's bust line. The firm swell of her breasts was hinted at, but subtly hidden by the soft folds of the fabric.

Peta continued to raise her eyes until hazel eyes met hazel eyes and she circumspectly examined the face that stared so seriously back at her. She tried to see herself as others did. What did they see in her? She didn't think she was startlingly beautiful, attractive maybe in a plain sort of way, perhaps. She had always thought her nose was too small. Yes, she admitted to herself; she had a pert nose. Someone had once called it cute, but Peta didn't think so. Her lips, although full, looked uninviting and Peta ran the tip of her tongue over their fullness, wondering why Beale found them so kissable. Her eyebrows were her best feature, she thought, well defined and thick, like her eyelashes which needed very little mascara to make them stand out. Her eyes, she supposed, weren't too bad if you liked hazel. She looked at herself in the mirror for another few seconds before she was able to bring her errant thoughts back under some semblance of control. If she didn't stop this particular train of thought, she was going to have herself convinced that she was the original plain Jane. She smiled a small smile at the woman standing next to her who, she could see, was openly watching her and the scrutiny she had been giving herself.

Shrugging her shoulders in her own defence, she asked quietly, "Will I do, Nancy? I so want to look beautiful for Beale."

"You'll do fine," Nancy said simply, "Beale is a very lucky man to have found someone who is beautiful on the inside as well as the outside," then she added for good measure, "That dress has just the right amount of provocative suggestion, don't you think? You look very demure, but totally alluring. I'm sure that when Beale sees you in this magical creation, he'll be driven quite mad with wanting you."

Peta had blushed profusely. She was touched by the other woman's words and although she found them to be slightly old fashioned, she wished with all of her heart for them to be true. She wanted Beale to want her for herself; to be driven wild with wanting her.

A gentle knock at the door had her spinning around in fright and she said in a hurried high pitched voice quite unlike her own, "Come in." Her heart was racing, for she thought she would see Beale coming through the door. She smiled a warm greeting when she saw her visitor was Beale's mother.

"Beale sent me in to tell you we're about ready to go. Do you need a hand with anything?" she asked casually, glancing about her satisfied Peta was nearly ready to leave. She added warmly, "You made a beautiful bride, dear. Your dress was so lovely. I don't think it could have been more perfect if it had been made for you."

"Thank you," Pete answered simply, then added, "and thank you. You've been so wonderful to me. If my mother was here, I doubt if she could have done more." On an impulse, Peta hugged the other woman, letting her know how grateful she was for her kindness.

"Why thank you, Peta. What a lovely thing to say." Nancy's eyes filled with tears and she dabbed at them with a delicate white linen handkerchief. Trying to lighten the conversation, which was in danger of turning into a repetition of thank-you's from them both, Peta smilingly said to her new mother-in-law, "Come on, help me with these things. You'll have me crying in a minute. I don't want Beale to see me with my makeup running down my face and with my eyes all teary or he might file for a divorce before the day is out." Her eyes were already bright with unshed tears at the unexpected kindness of her new mother-in-law.

"There's no chance of that, my dear. He's completely besotted with you. The poor boy doesn't know what day it is." She laughed as she walked towards the door carrying a handful of Peta's belongings, but then she stopped and turning to Peta with a serious expression on her face she said, "I want you to know how happy I am that Beale has married you. I wanted to officially welcome you into the family while we were by ourselves. I know it isn't at all necessary, but with Beale's father gone and all . . . with him not here to tell you himself . . . ," Shrugging her shoulders, she couldn't continue and Peta saw a fine mist of tears covering Nancy's eyes.

To be welcomed into the family like this meant everything to her. It meant she had a home, somewhere she belonged, and someone to whom she belonged. Peta followed Beale's mother from the room with a light-hearted feeling that she had not only gained a mother-in-law when she married Beale, but that she had gained a friend. Her heart went out to the other woman. She must miss her husband terribly.

Peta thought about the comment made so lightly concerning Beale's feelings for her. It would be wonderful if he was besotted with her. She couldn't deny that they seemed to generate a magical chemistry which flared between them whenever they kissed. On the occasions when they partook of this most pleasurable pastime, Peta was convinced that Beale was as affected as she was herself, feeling the attraction between them as strongly as she did.

A short time later saw them seated at the restaurant where Beale had made reservations prior to their wedding day. His mother was a reluctant third, telling them she didn't think it was appropriate for her to accompany them.

"What will people think," she told them self-consciously, "I should have stayed at the hotel."

"Nonsense," Peta told her, "we want you with us, don't we, Beale? This meal is the equivalent of a wedding reception." She looked across to Beale for confirmation, which he readily gave.

"But," he added lightly, "I draw the line at taking you on our honeymoon!" Peta glanced at him and saw the twinkle in his eyes as he imparted this last piece of information to his mother.

"You're impossible," the older woman told him while trying to hold back the hint of a smile that was tugging at the corners of her mouth.

Peta was trying hard to stop the blush that was infusing her face with colour as she thought about their wedding night. She fervently hoped that she wouldn't disappoint Beale when they made love.. He was probably very experienced and sure of himself when it came to making love while she . . .

"Hey," the man who was consuming all of her thoughts gently touched her arm, "A penny for them," he said, gazing deeply into her eyes. She sensed that he somehow realised that she had been thinking about him. Lately, all of her waking moments had centred on him.

He sensuously let his fingers roam over her hand, caressing the length of her fingers before he gently squeezed them, letting her know with his actions that he was far from immune from her brand of charms.

They didn't stay long over their meal. Beale's mother pleaded tiredness as she pushed herself away from the table telling them, "If you don't mind, I'll leave you now. It's been a big day and I'm totally exhausted. By the way," she added as another thought struck her, "will I see you in the morning before you leave?"

Beale answered casually, "I don't see why not. We haven't made any firm plans about when we'll leave, although I can't leave it very much longer before we head back. I want to take Peta to Deadman's Gorge. As an artist, I'm sure she'll appreciate the surrounding scenery, not to mention the story that goes with it."

"Oh yes, do take her!" Beale's mother said enthusiastically to him before she turned to tell Peta, "You'll love it there. It's one of my favourite places in the whole world. It's so very beautiful. The colours, the atmosphere . . . just beautiful."

Peta smiled at them both. "I'm sure I will."

Gathering up her handbag, Beale's mother told her as she prepared to leave, "Make sure you have your camera. Perhaps later you can recreate the scenes by putting them on canvas."

"Okay, Mum, enough already. Peta will see for herself when we arrive," Beale gently shooed his mother away with his hand, then belatedly asked her if she'd like him to accompany her to the taxi rank while she waited for a cab. Thoughts of Peta had driven every sane thought from his mind, even thoughts of looking after his mother.

"No, dear, I'll be fine. You attend to your new bride," she told him, gazing down fondly at Peta, who was once again trying to hide the colour that had risen to the surface of her cheeks.

Peta told them both hurriedly, "Actually, Beale, you can go with your mother. It will give me a chance to freshen up." Upon delivering these words to them both she stood up and walked resolutely towards the ladies room. which was near the kitchen entrance and strategically hidden behind some potted greenery.

"Alright. I won't be long," he said to her retreating back.

"Come on, mother," he said resignedly, taking his mother gently by the elbow and guided her towards the exit and ultimately the taxi rank. He secretly hoped there would be a cab waiting to whisk his mother away so that he could get back to his lovely bride. He loved his mother dearly, but for now he was impatient to have Peta all to himself. She looked so lovely, so alluring, he could hardly believe that she was finally his.

Putting his mother into the waiting taxi, he bent down and impulsively kissed her on the cheek. "Thank you for being so wonderful today, Mum, and for helping with the wedding. I'm sure Peta appreciated all that you did for her."

He stood back from the car as the driver prepared to depart. Just before the driver expertly manoeuvred the vehicle away from the curb, Beale's mother told him simply, "Be happy, Son."

Smiling his reassurance, Beale waited until the vehicle had disappeared from sight before he purposely strode back inside to their table. Peta had returned and was sitting waiting for him. She looks pale, he thought as he covered the short distance that separated them. It had certainly been a big day for her. Marrying someone on trust, hoping that the promises they'd made to each other wouldn't be broken, promising to bear his child, to honour the vows they had so recently taken. He vowed to himself that he would never break the trust that she had so willingly placed in him.

Not seeing any reason for them to linger over the remains of their meal that had been consumed long ago, Beale suggested to Peta, "Shall we go as well, unless you'd like another cup of coffee?"

"No, I'm fine," she stated, pushing her chair out from beneath her as she prepared to stand, showing an eagerness that she was far from feeling.

She returned his look and Beale thought he detected a slight look of apprehension that seemed to be quickly veiled, making him wonder if it had been there at all. Was she dreading their wedding night? He was certain he hadn't misunderstood the passion that had been steadily growing between them for the last two weeks. God, had it only been two weeks! Already he felt so at ease with the woman to whom he had given his heart. Of course, love hadn't been part of the bargain that they'd made with each other, but one couldn't help falling in love. These things just happened. He made a promise to himself that if Peta wasn't ready to consummate their marriage, then he would wait. He just hoped his need for her wouldn't override the resolution he was making with himself.

Beale ushered her before him into their suite in the local hotel he'd chosen. Peta's head was whirling from the pent up emotion of the last few days. Lowering her lashes, she found she couldn't look at him, lest she should give away the secret that was gnawing at her heart. She felt awkward, not really knowing what she should do. The large king-size bed seemed to dominate the room, making it extremely difficult to notice any of the other furnishings that the room provided. Swallowing nervously, her gaze rested momentarily on the piece of furniture and she smiled weakly to herself, thinking about the symbolic significance the bed represented. Unity, coming together as man and wife. Her face paled slightly as she thought about Beale and all that he represented in her life from this moment on.

"Peta?" Beale's eyes questioned her. His emerald green stare held her captive. She was mesmerised by the mounting desire she could detect blazing just below the surface of his consciousness.

Her breath caught in her throat, making breathing difficult, but she held his stare with a confidence that she was far from feeling as he devoured her with his eyes. Now was the moment of truth. All of her hopes and dreams for the future hinged on this single moment in time. Would she be able to uphold her part of the bargain and give herself to this man, knowing as she did he didn't return the love that so overpowered her every time she thought about him.

He hadn't tried to touch her and Peta was almost relieved when he suddenly turned away from her to start taking some toiletries from his suitcase, which had been placed on a small table along with hers at the end of the bed. Their cases had been brought to the room earlier in the day by Beale, who had then used the room to ready himself for the wedding.

Needing some extra time to collect her thoughts, Peta told him hastily, "I think I'll have a shower." She made a grab for her small overnight case, which held the belongings she would need, and made a hasty retreat towards the bathroom door. She added before closing the door on him, "I promise not to use all the hot water." Goodness, she was making small talk. *We just got married and I'm making small talk! What will he think of me*, but for the life of her, Peta didn't know what to do? Perhaps while she was showering, she would produce a gleam of inspiration ... something, anything to melt the ice that was steadily starting to form around the edges of her heart and driving a wedge between them. She hated herself for being so weak, but she told herself from the relative safety behind the locked door she needed to collect herself before she could present herself to her new husband.

If we'd been a normal couple, she told her reflection, *I wouldn't be feeling so awkward. We'd be talking, laughing, making plans.* Her heart longed to be linked with Beale, to have him utter the words she most wanted to hear.

Walking back into the room was difficult, but Peta managed this small task with a brightness she was far from feeling. She was feeling acutely self-conscious and altogether unsure of herself. Her night attire consisted of one slightly sexy garment that had been a last-minute purchase brought at Nancy's insistence. She had told her all young brides should have something with which to entice their husbands. Now she felt embarrassed and wished that she had opted for the nightgown of her choice, which had been pretty without any of the overriding sexual connotations that this gown envisaged. She had to grudgingly admit that her skin felt wonderful as the silken creation caressed her body, clinging to her womanly curves, leaving nothing to the imagination.

Beale was sitting in one of the many comfortable chairs that were placed strategically around the room. He was reading the local paper, which was supplied to every room. He didn't seem to be overly interested in the contents, a fact that was borne out when he immediately lowered the paper upon hearing Peta walk back into the room. He casually folded the pages over, putting them on the floor beside his chair.

"My turn, I think," he told her with a smile before he disappeared into the room that she had just vacated.

Peta felt the nerves in her stomach tighten as she watched him disappear through the door of the bathroom.

The door opened a few seconds later when Beale poked his head around the door to tell her warmly, "By the way, you look terrific in that getup."

Peta's heart leapt. She regarded him steadily, telling him in a voice that sounded strange to her ears, "Don't be long." She had made her decision.

He would never know the inner turmoil those few words had caused her love torn heart, but she knew this was to be a real marriage, real in every sense that a marriage should be and it had to start this very night.

Her heart was beating wildly as she sat waiting for Beale to finish in the bathroom. She looked around the room, needing something to do, wanting to calm her screaming nerves. It was at times like this when she was feeling stressful that she usually dragged out her paintings to put her emotions down on canvas, but all of her equipment, newly purchased, was safely packed away waiting to be transported out to the property.

Champagne! Peta thought purposely as she walked towards the small fridge that was set into the side of one wall, along with an assortment of shelves and benches. I think this occasion calls for champagne. She recalled Beale had ordered a bottle when he'd reserved the room earlier in the week. Perhaps if she had something to do, she wouldn't be so incredibly nervous.

When Beale walked back into the room a short time later, his hair was slicked back off his face and he looked newly shaved. Peta could smell his aftershave and breathed deeply, loving the musky aroma that was slowly permeating throughout the room.

"Mmm, you smell nice," she told him simply, and you look wonderful, she told herself. He was wearing a short robe over what looked like a pair of royal blue boxers. The robe was loosely knotted and Peta could see the mass of jet black hair that covered his chest. She had seen him before at the beach when they'd gone swimming, but tonight there seemed to be a special significance in gazing at the hard planes of his well-toned body.

He flashed her a quick smile before he told her, "A present from mum.

Peta's breath caught in her throat. "Likewise," she told him huskily. She hoped he couldn't detect the slight tremor that was present in her voice.

"Ah, I see you've found the champagne. I was going to suggest that we have a drink," he told her as he expertly dislodged the cork from the bottle before pouring them both a golden shaft of the bubbling liquid.

"To us," he told her, holding the sparkling drink up in a salute before raising the glass to his lips to leisurely take a small sip.

"To us," Peta repeated, following his lead. Beale had been so wonderful and she would be forever grateful for the space he had allowed her, but now she knew the time had come for them to be together. Her fears had to be forgotten and set aside.

"Shall we go to bed," Beale asked casually, putting his wine glass down onto the bench before turning to her for confirmation.

Peta merely nodded. She couldn't have spoken, for her heart was firmly lodged in her mouth, beating wildly. She could feel the nerves in her stomach tighten, and her mouth had gone dry. Now was the time to tell him that she . . . she . . .

"I thought like an idiot that you were shy. It never occurred to me you were a . . . ,"

"A virgin," Peta finished for him, "Yes, well I guess we're a dying breed with so many people opting to have sexual relationships these days."

She could see that Beale was clearly distressed by her outburst. "Don't say it like that. It's not a disease to want to keep your virginity until you marry, but why didn't you tell me," he asked her softly. He was holding Peta gently in the crook of his arm. She fitted perfectly, and he loved the feel of her against his bare skin. His voice held a slight tremor as he tried to bring his thoughts back to their conversation.

"I was embarrassed. I didn't know how to tell you. Anyway, the subject never came up, did it?" Peta told him frankly.

"No, I guess it didn't," he answered candidly, but he thought adamantly to himself if he had realised this beautiful woman lying next to him had been inexperienced in the ways of making love he would have approached their wedding night in a far different manner. A manner which would have helped her to overcome any fears that she might have harboured concerning their making love, for he could see now that she had indeed been nervous about their approaching nuptials.

"Are you angry?" Peta wanted to know, not quite knowing how to respond to him.

"Good heavens, no!" Beale exclaimed immediately. Bracing himself on one elbow, he gazed down into her lovely face in wonder, marvelling at how she could think him so callous as to be irked by the wonderful gift she had given him, the gift of herself. He continued more sedately, "It's just that if I'd known, I'd have been more . . . more . . .," he floundered as he tried to find the adequate words to explain how he was feeling without actually blurting out that he loved her. He didn't think now was the time to disclose that particular piece of information, but perhaps later, once they'd talked this thing through. He would have taken more time, been infinitely more careful. He felt like a complete brute, but the sight of her waiting for him had moved him to depths of passion that he hadn't felt with any other woman. He had wanted her with a burning intensity that had overwhelmed him completely. Rational thought had been left far behind as he'd taken her in his arms. She had looked so beautiful, and he had wanted her so badly.

"More what," Peta teased. She thought their lovemaking had been wonderful, but perhaps because of her inexperience she had disappointed him. Unexpected tears flooded her eyes as she remembered the closeness they had shared. Her body had responded willingly to his caresses, taking her on an unsurpassed journey of delight. Her nerve endings had vibrated and sung joyously and she remembered crying out with sheer delight, revelling in the glorious sensation that had coursed throughout her entire body leaving her spent, but, oh, so very contented. Peta's voice wavered as she told him contritely, "I'm sorry."

Beale surprised her by gathering her up into a strong embrace. He placed a tender kiss on her trembling lips. He could taste the saltiness of her tears as they ran freely down her pale cheeks.

"Sweetheart, you've got it all wrong. I'm the one who's sorry," he held up a commanding finger to silence her when she would have interrupted him, "I lost control. I should have been more careful, more patient. If I'd known it was your first time . . . ," he floundered feeling like a complete heel, then taking a deep breath he continued,

"Now, because of me and my complete lack of sensitivity I've probably turned you off men forever in my haste to make love to you." His deep masculine voice was tinged with sincere regret as he added remorsefully, "I hope I didn't hurt you too badly."

"Oh, Beale, please don't," she pleaded with him, wanting to ease the pain she could see lurking behind his beautiful emerald eyes. His forehead was etched in furrows as he gazed down at her. "You didn't hurt me . . . well maybe a little for a second or so," she told him as she remembered the initial thrust of his body when he had entered her for the first time, "but that was natural. I expected that, and it was alright. As for the other, you haven't turned me off men, quite the contrary. Your expertise has whetted my appetite for more of the same. Will you," she ran her tongue over lips that had suddenly gone very dry, feeling slightly embarrassed at having to ask this next question of him. She started again after taking a deep breath to fortify herself. "Could you, that is, would you show me . . . you know?" she finished lamely, feeling acutely embarrassed at having to ask her husband to instruct her in the art of making love.

"Consider it done," he told her softly before bringing his lips down to cover her own in a tender armistice, which was meant to strengthen the bond that was steadily starting to grow between them. They had all the time in the world and he planned to make the most of every second, showing his new wife the hidden delights that were theirs for the taking. It was all he could do to hold back the words of love he so wanted to adorn her with. Instead, he told her through lips that held a hint of a smile, "I've never met a virgin before. You're a fast learner, Jupiter Jacobs."

Peta thrilled at the use of his surname when it was linked to her own. She laughed softly up at him as she offered him her lips in a kiss that wasn't at all virginal. She was impatient for the lesson to start.

Seven days later, Peta walked through the front door of her new home. She had laughingly pleaded with Beale not to carry her over the threshold when he would have picked her up in the age old tradition and carried her into the house.

Looking around her with undisguised interest, Peta approved of the furnishings she saw. "This is a beautiful room, Beale. I love it."

"I thought you would. My great, great, great grandmother, Kathleen Jacobs, furnished the place soon after she was brought here as a blushing bride. For some reason every woman who has lived here since then has been happy to leave things as they are, but if you want to change anything, feel free to do so. This is your domain now." he told her simply. Coming to stand behind her, he drew her into the firm contours of his strong masculine body with his arms firmly holding her in place. His hands were casually caressing her stomach, and she arched herself into him, loving the feeling his touch always aroused within her.

Beale started nuzzling the side of her face, playfully at first, but when Peta offered him her neck, his caress became more serious and demanding. She turned in his arms to face him, wanting his lips to cover hers, which they did, immediately fusing them together in a passionate embrace which promised so much more.

"Boss, hey, boss, I'm glad you're back. I, oh, sorry, I didn't think you would be, that is, I . . . um, I didn't think . . . oh, it doesn't matter. I can come back later." The young man had started to back out of the door when Beale called him back into the room.

"Crawfish. Come back in. It's alright. I'd like you to meet my wife," Beale said casually to the young man who dutifully came back into the room. Peta could see that he appeared to be shy in front of her. She smiled across at him, hoping to put the young man at ease.

"Peta, this is Crawfish. Crawfish, this lovely lady is my wife, Peta," he said by way of introduction.

Crawfish merely nodded in her direction. He held his hat casually in his hand, but Peta knew instinctively that he'd accepted her. She wasn't going to push any of Beale's employees into a forced friendship, but would rather take the time for them to get to know her themselves. She fervently hoped that they'd all accept her. This station was like a small community, and it would be uncomfortable if she wasn't accepted by her husband's fellow workers.

"Hello," she said simply and left it at that. When Crawfish departed a short time later, she turned to Beale to ask inquisitively, "Crawfish?"

"His name is Tom Crawford. He picked up the name Crawfish because he has a mad passion for fishing."

"Oh," Peta said, accepting the simple explanation then asked with interest, "Are there many places around here where he could go fishing? I would have thought it was to dry to even catch a tadpole."

"You'd be surprised at the number of fishing holes that open up during the wet, but you're right though because for most of the year the waterholes dry up. Crawfish goes to the coast whenever he has time off and fishes there, apparently."

"How many other characters am I going to meet before this day is through?" she wanted to know.

"One or two I expect," he told her. "They'll all want to meet you. Does that pose any sort of problem for you, Mrs. Jacobs?"

"None that I can think of, although I'm a bit nervous."

"Why?" Beale wanted to know, "they're just ordinary people like you and me."

"I know, but I can't help feeling a little overwhelmed by it all. I mean, what if they don't like me?"

"I'll sack them," Beale told her instantly, not quite able to hide the small smile that was playing around the corners of his lips.

"Okay," she answered jauntily, "I'll hold you to that."

"Done," he told her.

The shrill ring of the phone stopped any more banter between them. Peta was pulled along at a leisurely pace down a short hallway, which took them to the side of the house. Beale opened the door and walked into the room to reveal an office of sorts. He reached for the phone and put it casually to his ear.

"Hello, Beale here," he said, then listened to the voice on the other end of the line, smiling at whatever was being said to him. "Well, I'm sorry about that, but if I didn't grab her when I did she might have changed her mind and broken my heart."

Peta looked up at him, knowing he was being questioned about their hasty marriage. They had agreed to tell everyone that they'd been seeing each other for almost a year. It saved a lot of embarrassing questions about why she agreed to marry him on such short notice. She wasn't prepared to answer those questions, even to herself.

Beale looked at his watch before saying, "Give us about half an hour then and we'll be down." He smiled at whatever was being said before tacking on, "Righto, see you then."

"Do you feel up to a bit of a do? The boys got word we were coming home and have put on an afternoon tea for you. I feel I should warn you though I've never known them to do anything like this before, so heaven only knows what we'll find when we get down there. With Mum still being away ... maybe I should ring them back and tell them you're tired," he stated, and actually started to reach for the phone.

"Don't you dare. They'll think I don't want to meet them. I'm sure anything they've done will be fine. Hasn't anyone ever told you it's the thought that counts." She thought it was sweet of the men to go to the trouble of doing this for her.

"Well, if you're sure."

He didn't sound at all convinced and Peta couldn't help asking him, "There won't be any naked women jumping out of wedding cakes or anything, will there?"

"I don't really know," he told her candidly, but he certainly hoped not. Apart from his mother, the men weren't used to having any females around, except for the odd occasion when he'd invited female companions to the homestead. Some of the men were married, but their wives had opted to live in Alice Springs, which was the closest major town being directly west of the property. Maybe now that Peta was here, the other women might agree to live here on the station. He had discussed the subject with her during the week because he was worried that she might pine for female companionship when he was away from the homestead. He hoped the men would remember to watch their language while Peta was in their midst. There wasn't one man on the place that he didn't trust completely with his life, but they were a rough bunch and he knew what they were capable of when they let their hair down at the end of a long day.

After showering and changing her clothes, Peta was ready to go. She couldn't stop the nervous fluttering that had settled into the pit of her stomach at meeting the people she would be sharing her life with on a daily basis.

"You look beautiful," Beale told her, walking into their bedroom. "The men haven't got a chance in hell of escaping your charms. And you smell so good." He bent down close to her ear and drew in a deep breath, expelling it slowly, loving the scent of her and the passionate memories it evoked of her writhing in his arms when they made love.

"Come on," he said with a noticeable catch in his deep voice, "we'd better get going before I change my mind and keep you here all to myself."

Peta wasn't sure just what she'd been expecting when she walked into the men's mess hall, but what greeted her took her completely by surprise.

The room was full of men, about twenty in all, all of whom were well groomed with their hair slicked back off clean-shaven faces. Their clothes, although casual, were immaculate.

Wooden collapsible tables had been set up across one wall and had been laden with a variety of foods. A banner which read Welcome Home Beale and Peta had been hung above the middle table. Peta was touched by all the trouble she knew the men must have gone to, trying to make her feel welcome. A record player had been placed against another wall and next to it there was a collection of tapes, vinyl records and some CD's.

Beale introduced her to everyone. They were all very polite and well-mannered, making Peta believe that they'd been told to be on their best behaviour. She hadn't a hope of remembering everyone's name and apologised to them all, telling them she'd need a bit of time to remember what name went with what man.

Someone handed her a glass of white wine and gave Beale a beer. This seemed to show that the party was to begin, for after that everybody moved around the room talking to different people about station matters or any topic that interested them. All were mindful of their manners, and Peta didn't hear one foul word during the entire time she was there.

Beale sat with her at one of the tables that had been strategically placed around the room. The men came up to him, filling him in on what had been happening while he'd been away. Each of them nodded to her or said a quick hello, but they didn't engage her in any conversation

"Blackrock Downs is closer to Alice Springs than it is to Longreach, although both places are accessible to us either by plane or by car. We have a few married men on the place, but their wives prefer to live in the city rather than live here on the property. We've set up a working roster where the men have ample free time to visit their wives regularly if they choose to."

"If they choose to," Peta repeated, slightly dumbfounded. She couldn't imagine being parted from Beale, even for a little while. "How many of them are married?"

"Eight, I think."

"Why do they live apart? Is it because there's no accommodation for them here on the station?" Peta asked, wondering yet again how anyone could choose to live apart from their spouse. She couldn't see the sense in getting married if you were going to live the life of a single person.

"For the first part, I think it's because Blackrock is so isolated. Our closest neighbours are two hundred kilometres away. Second, I have offered on several occasions to make accommodation available to the married men, but so far there have been no takers to my proposal."

"Which is?" Peta prompted, wanting to know more.

"I offered to have bungalows built if anyone wanted to bring their wives out to Blackrock. Now that you're here, I'm going to insist on it. I want you to have some female company."

"But why? I keep telling you I'll be fine. I like my own company, Beale," she declared, placing a hand on his arm.

"I don't want you to get bored. Will some female company be that bad? Most women would be tearing their hair out, screaming at me to take them away to the delights of the city."

"I'm not most women, I'm me," she told him lightly. She was determined that she wasn't going to ask who the woman was who had yearned for the city lights, but vivid images of the blonde woman swam before her eyes.

"And you don't know how happy that makes me feel," Beale sighed as he took in the beauty of his lovely wife as she sat quietly next to him.

One older man who had been sitting with a group of men suddenly stood up and walked across to where they were sitting. "Do you mind if I sit down, Missus, and have a chat with you? The rest of the mob are too shy for their own good. They need to get out more."

"No, please do," Peta told him, happy to have someone to talk to. Beale had been talking to her, but she so wanted to get to know the rest of the men. She knew it would be the wrong thing to do to go and talk to them. She had to be patient and wait until they came to her.

"So you finally got this fella to the altar. Good for you. He's not a bad catch, I suppose. You caught him young enough so that you can train him up in all the proper ways. Some of these other blokes, well, I reckon someone as pretty as you wouldn't give them the time of day," he said, looking at Peta to see what her reaction would be to this line of questioning.

"Mm, he's not a bad catch. You're probably right about training him though, but so far I can't say that I've had any major problems." Peta looked across at Beale and saw that he was smiling. He didn't seem to mind in the least that he was the topic of conversation. He was content to be silent and let the two of them take control of the conversation. It was good that Vic had come over to talk to her. He knew it wouldn't be long before a few of the others did the same, and then the ice would be broken.

"So, how did you meet our roving Romeo?" Vic wanted to know. Peta noticed a few heads turned towards them with interest at this question.

She launched into the story that had, in reality, only taken place a couple of weeks ago. "We were both broken down on the side of the highway, or at least Beale's car was broken down. Mine had a flat tyre. It was raining, and I didn't want to get out in the rain. He came up to the window and frightened the life out of me by asking for a lift. I told him if he'd fix my puncture, I'd give him a lift."

"Ah, that's our boy. I suppose he swept you off your feet," Vic asked with enthusiasm, smiling broadly at Beale.

"No, not exactly. At least not straight away," Peta elaborated. She didn't want to spoil Vic's romantic fantasy, but the temptation to tell the half truthful story got the better of her.

Vic's look of bewilderment brought a smile to her lips. She gazed at Beale, knowing he wouldn't mind. She knew he realised what she was going to say. He shrugged his shoulders, letting her know it was okay.

"Actually, he went to sleep."

This statement brought a roar of laughter from the men in the room, all of whom had been listening to the conversation with rapt attention.

"He didn't!" Vic exclaimed, staring at Beale, wanting conformation to this piece of news.

Beale nodded, telling them all he'd been tired. "Anyway, I made up for it later, the next time we met."

"Really, how?" they all wanted to know.

"I'm not going to tell you all of my secrets. Suffice to say, I got my girl and convinced her to marry me."

That would have been a story Peta would have liked to hear as well. She hoped with all of her heart that their story would have a happy ending.

"You could have knocked us over with a feather when we heard the news," another one of the men told her. "We didn't know Beale was serious about anyone in particular. He always had so many girls chasing after him when he was younger, but he never seemed interested in any of them. We should have realised when he kept hot-footing it off to the city that he was on a mission."

"I guess I came along at the right time," Peta told them. Images of the blonde woman she'd seen Beale escorting in Rockhampton flooded her mind, forcing her to momentarily frown. Luckily nobody seemed to notice except for Beale, who wondered what thoughts had passed through her mind, causing her to change her facial expression, however briefly.

"What did you do, that is, what work did you do before you got married?" Someone asked her.

"I had my own business. I ran an arts and craft shop in Rockhampton."

The floodgates had opened, and the questions came one after the other, with everyone wanting to know about her background. Peta happily answered all of their questions, glad to be talking. It meant a lot to her that she'd been accepted by the men who Beale classed not only as colleagues, but friends as well.

Later that night, as she was getting ready for bed, Peta thought of the past week and the delights she had shared with her new husband. She wished she could tell him how happy he made her, not only sexually, for he knew she was well satisfied with that side of their marriage, but there were other things.

They were friends as well as lovers, and that meant everything to her. She felt she could tell him anything except the one thing that mattered most to her, her all-consuming love for him. She fervently prayed that one day in the not too distant future she'd be able to share her love with him as well.

Chapter Six

THEIR INTENDED SIGHTSEEING TRIP that would finally bring them back to Blackrock Downs had been abandoned when they had decided, by mutual consent, to return to the beach house for the rest of their honeymoon.

"We have the rest of our life for you to show me the beauty of the outback," Peta told him candidly, "but how often will we get the chance to visit the beach?"

"True, I suppose," Beale agreed, coming to sit beside her on his bed, which they now shared in the master bedroom, "as long as you're sure."

Her memory slipped back to the day they'd gone back to the beach house, the day after their marriage. Peta had been concerned that her lack of knowledge about the outback and the life she was about to embark on would present Beale with a problem once they reached the station.

She remembered asking him. "I mean, how is it going to look if I can't tell the difference between a blade of grass and a weed. Heck, I can't even ride a horse. Actually, I might even be a little bit scared of them. Everyone's going to think you've married a 'townie'!"

Beale had hooted with laughter at her misgivings. "I did marry a townie," he had told her, "but a very attractive, very sexy townie at that. I can see every man on the place falling over themselves wanting to tell you the difference between a blade of grass and a weed, not to mention the difference between a bull and a steer and so on and so forth."

She didn't believe for a second that her appearance at the station would raise anything but a casual glance once the men came to know her. But, she thought, I will have to learn all the day-to-day operations that go towards running a busy property the size of Blackrock Downs. Beale wouldn't always be available to answer the endless questions she was sure she'd have for him over the course of the next few weeks, until she became accustomed to her new home.

"A steer and a bull," she said to him knowingly, wanting to share her limited knowledge with him, "I already know what they are, they're boy cows."

Beale's grin lit up his entire face, and his beautiful emerald eyes danced with merriment as he advanced towards her. "Is that so?" he told her as he gathered her up into his capable arms and carried her down the hallway towards the bedroom, where he placed her gently on the bed. "I think, my beautiful wife, that you need an anatomy lesson from someone who just happens to be an expert on the subject of bulls and steers."

Peta's remark had been stupid and light-hearted, but it had been the prelude to a beautiful night of lovemaking when he had further introduced her body too many more hidden delights which had resulted in the complete abandonment of any barriers which might have existed between them. He had also shown her how to please him, how to touch him. Peta had willingly learned, letting her hands roam freely over his heated body until he had cried out in the throes of passion, needing to be one with her.

Now, a week later, she felt perfectly at ease in his company, trusting him completely.

"What are you smiling about?" Beale had walked into the bedroom. His only covering was a towel which was knotted loosely at his side and slung low over his masculine hips. He exuded sex appeal, and Peta's breath caught in her throat as she feasted her eyes hungrily upon him.

She knew her need for him was mirrored in her eyes so she simply said, telling him softly through barely parted lips, "I was thinking of making love with you. Make love to me, Beale."

Peta loved their life together at the station. Although she'd only been here a few days, life had been idyllic. She had taken over the running of the station office, helping Beale with his personal mail. Before this, he had struggled through miles of paperwork, often working well into the night to keep abreast of the ever-growing pile that continued to accumulate on his desk. Some of the letters he received positively amazed her, and she was sure she could help with their speedy dispersal. In her own business she'd had to deal with similar things, although not on such a grand scale.

"You might want to talk with Vic; he handles most of the station correspondence. He writes all the cheques and handles any problems that arise concerning any pay hassles we might have. Everything is done mostly by computer nowadays and electronic banking is a blessing, but every now and again we seem to have a hiccup when we lose service."

"Do you think he'd mind if I helped?" she asked, concerned that the other man might resent her intrusion into an area that he saw as his own personal domain. She was sitting on a stool in the bathroom, watching Beale as he shaved. She loved to watch him perform this menial task.

"I know he won't. He's been asking me to pull one of the boys in from the outcamp so he can have some help. The trouble is nobody really wants to come in and I can't say that I blame them."

"Well then, that settles it. I'll do it. I can't keep sitting around doing nothing, Beale. I'm starting to feel positively lazy."

"Okay, but don't overdo it. I didn't bring you out here to work your fingers to the bone," he told her, stooping down to kiss the tip of her nose.

She breathed in the pure male scent of him, loving the tantalising aroma that filled her nostrils. Putting her hands casually around his neck, she kept him a willing captive as she lightly kissed his lips, running her tongue sensuously over his open mouth.

"Woman," he groaned as he looked down into Peta's upturned face, so close to his own. He could see her mounting desire and knew in that instant that he was lost.

When Beale finally left for the day, he was grumbling good-naturedly that he was late for work yet again. He stood at the doorway to their bedroom and blew her a quick kiss. Peta smilingly asked him to come and give it to her in person. She had no idea how alluring she looked, lying back against the pillows, perfectly at ease with her nakedness. Her long brown hair was tousled and splayed out around her head. She was surrounded by the aftermath of their torrid lovemaking, and Beale thought she'd never looked lovelier. He was sorely tempted and would have liked nothing better than to go back to her, to gather her into his strong arms and love her.

Peta was conscious that every time they made love, there was a distinct possibility that she could become pregnant. Their child could be growing inside of her this very minute. She placed her hands protectively across her stomach and gently massaged the area where she knew her child would start its young life. She knew instinctively that Beale would love their child, for he was a good man. Perhaps this would have to be enough for her. Their child would also receive the love that she couldn't openly give to her husband.

It saddened her to think that Beale didn't return the love she felt for him, that he wasn't even aware that she harboured such an all-consuming, deep burning love for him which had completely overwhelmed her. She found it difficult to believe that he hadn't guessed her secret. Perhaps he thinks he's created a sex maniac and is happy to leave it at that, she thought ruefully. Their lovemaking was so beautiful, and Peta wondered if all couples shared the magic that she'd found with Beale.

After taking a leisurely shower, Peta made herself a cup of tea as she usually did and took it into the drawing room, where she sat down on one of the elaborately upholstered settees to decide just what her plans would be for today.

She looked around the room and wondered how this lovely furniture would stand up to the rigors that a young family would subject it to. Having an avid passion for antiques, she had become interested in the beautiful period furniture that filled every room of the homestead. She would have to teach her children to have a healthy respect for the contents of this house. She wanted them to grow up appreciating who they were, but also where they'd come from. She wanted them to appreciate the struggle and the hardship that had taken place so that they could someday take over the reins of Blackrock Downs when their time came. They were going to know that their heritage wasn't something to be taken for granted. Beale agreed with her and had laughed when she had told him she'd like a large family.

Beale had told her a little of the history concerning his ancestors. Peta had been fascinated and had listened with rapt attention when he'd told her about his great, great, great grandmother, Kathleen Isobel Jacobs, who had been the first woman to be brought to this house as a new bride over one hundred and twenty years ago.

"My great, great, great grandfather started the property with just one hundred head of cattle and forty acres of land. Apparently he sent to England for a wife and married her when her ship docked in Sydney. He wanted sons to run the property when he died and to continue the family name. He hadn't met his wife, he only knew her name, but he was prepared to take a wife if it meant preserving his heritage."

"But I thought you said your great, great, great grandmother was the first woman to come into this house." Peta asked him, thinking she must have misunderstood.

"That's right, she was. This house was built for her. The other one was destroyed by fire. It was waiting for her when she returned here as his wife," he told her, amused at her avid interest in his ancestors.

"How do you know if all of this information is correct? Is there a diary somewhere? It would be lovely to know the thoughts and dreams of your forebears," she said with a heartfelt sigh.

"You're a true romantic, but yes, I have a journal, or rather Mum has it. When she comes home, ask her for it, then you can thumb through it any time your heart desires. There are supposed to be others, but they have either been lost or destroyed because I've never seen them. Mum told me when I was a child that there's supposed to be a secret hiding place close to the house, but I think that's a story that's been passed down from generation to generation and has been distorted in the process of the telling. The story goes that my great, great, great grandfather used to beat her when he'd get into one of his drunken rages. She would go to this place to hide from him."

Peta was silent as she took in Beale's words. Her heart went out to his long dead relative. How sad to have to hide, to fear for your life. She wondered if the woman eventually found peace or did she die never knowing the love of a good, decent man.

"Hey, where did you go to? You were miles away."

"Oh!" Peta exclaimed in embarrassed bewilderment as she looked up at him. She was horrified when her eyes filled with unshed tears.

Beale stared down at her in amazement when he saw the fine mist of tears that she was trying unsuccessfully to hide from him. He laughed tenderly, pulling her into his strong embrace, holding her close.

Peta loved the hardness of him and burrowed her body closer against the steely strength of him. She couldn't understand why she was reacting so strangely. It was a sad story, yes, but as Beale had said, it had happened long ago. She was grateful that he hadn't made fun of her tears. She thought contentedly to herself, this is where I belong, where I want to stay.

Peta was delighted when Beale's mother walked into the homestead the next morning. She'd been sorting the mail and was looking for an excuse to take a break.

"Nancy!" she exclaimed happily, "How wonderful to see you." She came around the table to give her mother-in-law a big heartfelt hug. "Come into the kitchen and I'll make us a cup of tea. You can tell me what you've been doing."

"Well, there's no need to ask you how married life is treating you. You are positively glowing, my dear," the other woman stated, happy to see that Peta seemed to have settled into station life. She knew some women couldn't adapt to the loneliness and the great stretches of emptiness.

She hoped her news wouldn't mar that happiness, for she could see a dark cloud looming on the horizon.

"I love it here. I couldn't see myself being anywhere else," Peta told her honestly. "Does Beale know you're back?" He would be happy to see his mother, for they seemed to be bound with a powerful bond. This pleased Peta, for she wished the same thing for her own children.

"No, he doesn't. I was going to suggest that we go down to the stockyards. There's something I think he should know."

"Is it anything I should know," Peta said light heartedly, thinking the problem was station business.

"I hope not. No, this is one problem that Beale has to deal with himself."

Peta accepted the fact that Nancy didn't want to tell her, but she fervently hoped the news had something to do with falling cattle prices and not a certain member of the opposite sex. Hopefully, Beale would tell her if there was any trouble.

"What has Beale shown you of the property? Did you get the chance to go out to Deadman's Gorge on your way home?" Nancy wanted to know.

"Actually, I've seen very little of the place. Beale has been so incredibly busy since we got back. I haven't wanted to bother him. He has suggested that we go for a picnic in a few days. He said he has to go out to check on something or other, but for the life of me, I can't remember what it was." Peta told Nancy as she handed her a mug of steaming hot tea.

"I thought Beale was going to show you the gorge as a part of your honeymoon trip?"

"He was, but we decided to stay at the beach. We caught a commercial flight from Rockhampton out to Longreach and from there we were able to hitch a ride on the mail plane which dropped us at the airstrip on the property."

While they were driving down to the yards, Peta took the opportunity to ask Nancy about Kathleen Jacobs and found that her mother-in-law was able to fill in a few of the gaps with regard to the life of the other woman.

"She must have been a fascinating woman," Peta remarked, looking about her with interest as she always did when she had occasion to leave the homestead. "I don't know why, but I feel so drawn to her somehow." She directed her glance towards Nancy, wanting to see the reaction this remark had on her mother-in-law.

"You have kindred souls, my dear," Nancy told her simply.

At Peta's look of total ignorance she explained, "Kathleen Jacobs was a sensitive, sweet, generous woman. You share those same qualities with her, Peta. I hope my son appreciates the treasure he's found in you and cherishes you as he should."

Although Peta didn't comment on Nancy's statement, it stayed with her and she wondered idly if anything had happened to make the other woman wonder about their relationship. She bit her lip as she thought of the possible reasons that Nancy could have and wondered briefly if she had somehow stumbled across the circumstances of their marriage.

Peta found it interesting to see how the men spent their day. Although she hadn't been any further than the station outbuildings since she'd been here, she still found there was plenty to see. Beale had promised to take her to one of the many outcamps, and she was looking forward to going with him.

Today some of the men were working close to the homestead on what they classed as purely mundane tasks, like fixing one of the station trucks that had broken an axle. Beale employed a full-time mechanic, telling her the property couldn't run efficiently without a fully qualified mechanic.

"Hey, Peta." Recognising Crawfish's voice, Peta turned, giving him a welcoming smile once he'd covered the short distance that separated them.

"Hello, Crawfish. I thought you were going out to number nine bore for a couple of days?"

"Beale brought me back in with the truck. I'll probably drive it back out later."

"Okay. Come and see me when you get back."

"Will do," he responded cheerfully before he headed over towards one of the many sheds that made up the maintenance area of the station.

Crawfish had gotten over his initial shyness that he had at first felt when she'd been around, and they had started the beginnings of a close friendship.

He was a lanky young man with shoulder-length blonde hair that was usually worn pulled back into a ponytail when he was working.

Peta had learned from Beale that Crawfish had been sent out to Blackrock as a last resort by concerned parents who had been extremely worried about his future.

"It's the same old story. He'd just finished high school. He was mixing with the wrong crowd and was getting into trouble. His parents saw an advertisement we were running for staff and they wrote to me. The rest, as they say, is history."

"So that means he came out here when he was about seventeen?" Peta's heart went out to Crawfish. She was glad the gamble that his parents had taken had paid off, for their son had turned out to be quite a likeable character.

Beale nodded, and then added while trying to suppress a slight smile, "So next time you go jumping on that motor bike with him to go roaming around the place, be aware that you could be in the presence of a potential thug. He might try to mug you."

"You're such a poor liar," Peta told him, responding to the mirth in his voice. She knew that if Beale had any misgivings about Crawfish, he would forbid her to go with him.

Crawfish was teaching her to ride a motorbike. She was getting very adept at handling the gear changes that were necessary to keep the bike in motion. She was very proud of the progress she was making.

Next, she was going to learn to ride on one of the station horses. Beale was going to teach her. He had already taken her down to the stables and had introduced her to the horse she would ride; a big gray gelding named Fagan. Peta had questioned Beale about the name, stating uncertainly that she thought the name Fagan had an

Irish connotation, which meant 'little fiery one'. Surely he wouldn't expect her to ride a horse that could throw her. The animal had looked to be huge, and Peta had wondered if she could overcome her fear, but she was certainly going to try. If Beale thought she could do it, then that was good enough for her. She trusted him completely, but she was reassured when he explained the origin of the animal's name.

Beale told her that Fagan was an acronym. The letters in the name stood for Falling Asleep Going Absolutely Nowhere, hence Fagan for short. He was the perfect mount for a beginner, being completely trustworthy and vice free.

The men had totally accepted her now, and several of them waved to her from across the compound. Vic walked past her and winked at her casually saying, "G'day Missus," in his broad Australian accent, "Beale's just over there." He jerked his head towards the shed before he continued on his way.

Peta found she had a soft spot for Vic. She had correctly labelled him a true larrikin. She had formed the habit of visiting him down at the mechanic's shop most days. He'd produce a packet of biscuits and his best mug so she could have a cup of tea and they'd settle down and have a chin-wag, as he put it. He was a wealth of information about life on the station, having lived and worked on the property for most of his life. He had arrived here forty years ago as a young man looking for work when Beale's father had been in charge and had, since that time, made Blackrock Downs his home.

Peta glanced in Beale's direction, seeking him out. How perfect my world would be if only he loved me, she thought as she watched him. He meant everything to her, filling her with love, happiness, contentment . . . in fact, everything she had ever wanted out of life, but he also filled her with a terrible sadness.

Feeling he was being watched, Beale stopped working and cast a casual glance in her direction. She saw him smile as he beckoned for her to join him. He was covered with dust and the sweat on his face had turned the dirt there to grime, but to Peta he looked wonderful.

"Hello, wife," he greeted her when she had covered the short distance to where he stood waiting for her.

"Hello," Peta answered, revelling in the thrill of hearing this simple term of endearment from him.

"Have you come to look over the family fortune? Remember the things I told you before you go wandering away from the house."

He had been adamant that she realised the danger she'd place herself in if she was to get lost. The outback was a huge place, and she was very insignificant as far as Mother Nature was concerned.

"I remember. Your mother brought me down. She arrived this morning. She wants to talk to you about something, but she wouldn't tell me what it was." Looking at Beale, she could tell he was in the dark as well.

"Mum's home. Good, now you'll have some female company, somebody else to talk to. And here I was thinking you'd come down especially to see me." He wiped his forearm across his forehead again, leaving another dirty smear in its wake.

"I wish you'd stop worrying about me having female company. I like being by myself. I'm sure your mother won't want to baby-sit me all the time. Anyway, once my gear arrives I won't want to talk to anyone, I'll have too much to do, and who said that I didn't want to see you," she beamed up at him thoroughly enjoying the banter that was passing between them. She loved it when he flirted with her.

Before she realised what he was going to do, he put an arm around her waist and gently pulled her closer to his side.

Peta glanced up at him expectantly, knowing he was going to kiss her so she wasn't at all surprised when he dropped a quick kiss onto her upturned lips, much to the amusement of his men who were working nearby. They offered up catcalls and made a few jokes about his not being able to make it through the day without a Peta break.

"Get back to work," he ordered them, knowing full well that his request would be totally ignored. He added, "Can't a man kiss his wife without being heckled."

To Peta he said, "See what I have to put up with," but she knew that every man who worked on Blackrock Downs thought the world of Beale and his mother.

"Come with me," he told her and grabbing her hand he took her into the small galvanised tin shed that stood directly behind them. "I want to show you something I think you'll be interested in. I was going to come up to the house and get you."

Peta thought he was taking her into the privacy of the shed to kiss her, so she followed him willingly. Rampant anticipation coursed throughout her body as she thought of his kisses.

But it wasn't kisses that Beale wanted to share with her. But an assortment of boxes and crates that were full of painting materials and old canvasses, plus several other things that Peta couldn't see.

"Look at all this. I'd forgotten they were here. There hasn't been anyone here who was interested enough to go through all of this mess. It looks like it should be on the junk heap." Beale looked back at her to gauge her reaction to the boxes and crates that had been carelessly stacked at the back of the shed.

"Who did they belong to?" she wanted to know, going down on her knees so she could get a better look at the contents of the carton closest to her.

"Kathleen Jacobs. She must have dabbled in a bit of painting when she had the time," Beale told her casually as he kicked over one of the canvasses with the tip of his boot to reveal an oil painting that was in urgent need of some tender loving care in order to restore it to its original magnificence.

"Beale!" she scolded him. "Don't do that. You'll ruin it. It's absolutely wonderful."

"It looks ruined already," he told her, looking at the painting again, trying to see it through fresh eyes, but to him it still looked as if it should be on the rubbish heap.

"No, it can be restored. It just has one hundred years of accumulated dirt on it," she said absently as she glanced at the rest of the boxes. "Do you know if all of these are her work?"

"As far as I know."

"How wonderful. She was a brilliant artist. Just look at those colours and how she's used them to their best advantage."

"If you say so," he stated simply, not really seeing anything to be excited about.

Peta smiled up at him, then gave him her hand, wanting him to help her to her feet. "Just wait until I fix them. Then you'll see what I mean."

When she was finally standing next to him, she reached up and planted a kiss onto his mouth, wanting to thank him for showing her the paintings.

"How wonderful," she said again, overwhelmed by the find. She put her arms around Beale's neck and planted a succession of kisses along his neck as a further thank you.

"Now that's more like it," he told her, kissing her with enthusiasm. Peta laughed against his lips, asking him joyfully if there was anything else he wanted to show her before she left.

"Talk like that can get you into a lot of trouble, Missus, with this little ol' country boy," he said casually, running his hands slowly down the centre of her back until they rested lightly on her softly rounded bottom. Applying some slight pressure, he brought her into intimate contact with his hard body.

Peta wantonly ground herself against him, loving the hardness of his body as it merged against her own supple softness. She was rewarded when she heard a slow groan of pure pleasure escape from his lips. Kissing him slowly, she introduced her tongue into his unresisting mouth and probed its soft contours. She could taste the strong male scent of him and knew she should try to stop, but she was powerless to put a halter onto her emotions, for they seemed to have developed a mind of their own when it came to this man standing here so enticingly in front of her.

"Peta, we have to stop. This isn't the time, or the place." A husky voice sounded slightly disjointed in her ear. Then she was pushed gently away from his body as he reluctantly stepped back from her, putting a bit of distance between them. Peta would never know how much of a concentrated effort it had taken for him to put a stop to the pleasurable feelings she had unleashed on his more than willing body.

Looking up into Beale's face with eyes that were glazed with unspent passion, Peta could see her own expression mirrored in his eyes. They were filled with the same urgent wanting as her own.

Taking a deep, shuddering breath, Peta tried to pull herself together, and she smiled ruefully at Beale across the short distance that separated them. He seemed to be in the same predicament and was trying to bring his laboured breathing under some semblance of control. Words weren't necessary, for they both knew what the other was thinking. If they hadn't come to their senses, or rather if Beale hadn't had the sense to call a halt to their lovemaking, they would have made love right here in the shed and be blowed with the consequences of being interrupted by his men.

When Beale walked into the homestead later that afternoon he was carrying a compact bundle of fur which he presented to Peta, placing it carefully onto her lap.

"Oh!" She exclaimed as she picked the tiny animal up to look adoringly into its cute puppy face. "It's beautiful. Is it for me?"

"She's for you," he told her. Station life was sometimes cruel, and these things happened from time to time. He'd known that Peta would take the pup, showing it love and compassion.

"Does she have a name?" she wanted to know as she followed him into the bedroom where he had started to strip off his dust covered clothes.

"No," he answered.

"Good. I'll call her Jolly." Peta buried her face into the animal's soft fur. As a child she had owned a dog called Jolly, and for some reason this little one reminded her of her other pet. She looked like she was part kelpie and part cattle dog. Peta instantly loved her.

After his shower, Beale announced to her that his mother wanted to see him. She had specifically asked him if he would come over to her place and he had reluctantly agreed, but he didn't think much of his mother's timing and had told her so, saying he had wanted to spend his time with his wife.

Wanton thoughts of Peta had filled his mind for most of this very long day since their passionate embrace in the shed earlier in the day. Longing for Peta was becoming a pastime with him, and he despaired of ever being able to share this secret with her. There were times when he felt she returned his love, but he wondered if he was confusing sexual satisfaction with intimacy.

Peta couldn't understand how a day could start out so perfectly and yet disintegrate into one of the worst days she could ever remember living through.

When Beale had arrived home the night before after visiting his mother, she could tell that his mind was clearly on other matters. That made her feel irritable, for he had opted not to share his feelings with her. She wanted to ask him what was wrong, but she chose not to, thinking that if he wanted her to know, he would tell her. They were supposed to be equal partners in this marriage. She had thought that meant during the bad times as well.

She knew with certainty that the news had something to do with Nancy's wanting to see him. The thought was driven home to her that if they were truly a loving couple instead of two individuals trying to live this foolish charade, he would probably not have hesitated in sharing his news with her, however unsavoury it might be. Isn't that what other husbands and wives do when they encounter a problem, she told herself sadly? Am I always going to be locked out of his thoughts whenever problems arise? Beale had told her they would be partners in this marriage sharing everything and as far as she was concerned, that meant the bad times as well.

Walking away from the homestead with Jolly to keep her company, Peta didn't have an actual destination in mind. She went for a walk most days, usually keeping the homestead in sight.

Jolly scampered ahead of her, happily chasing her tail. She was full of the joy of life and certainly seemed to be living up to her name. Peta smiled at her antics, wishing life could be that simple. They were approaching a small outcrop of rocks that were partially hidden by some overgrown brown thorn bushes and bracken. Peta wanted to give the area a wide berth, conscious of the fact that she could stumble upon a snake if she went too close, but Jolly had different ideas. The pup ran up to the outcrop and forced herself between the bushes. Peta was horrified to see her disappear into the undergrowth.

"Jolly," she exclaimed nervously, "please come out!"

Her cries were in vain for Jolly ignored her or, thought Peta perturbed, perhaps having made her way in, she wasn't able to get back out. Oh dear, what was she to do. She looked about her, hoping that she'd see someone to help her, but the surrounding landscape was devoid of any life. She was agitated that help wasn't at hand. If Jolly was to be saved, she'd have to do it herself.

Cursing the little dog for making her go in after her, Peta warily parted the bushes. Her heart was hammering against her ribs and she looked fearfully from side to side as she slowly made her way deeper into the undergrowth towards the rocks. In the back of her mind she could hear Beale's warning about taking care of herself, but she couldn't leave Jolly alone. If a snake was to bite her, she knew it would probably be fatal, for she wouldn't have enough time to get help for herself.

She could hear Jolly somewhere up ahead of her. She certainly didn't seem to be in any trouble for Peta could hear her playfully barking in the distance, but please, God, don't let it be a snake or a spider that has her attention.

"Jolly," she scolded, "you and I have to have a little talk about doing what you're told."

Total amazement covered Peta's face as she parted the last few branches that were obstructing her way to reveal a small opening in the rocks directly in front of her.

"It's a cave!" she said in bewilderment as she cautiously peered into the semi-darkness. Should she go in? Curiosity had certainly gotten the better of her, and she slowly crept forward on her hands and knees, keeping a wary eye on the ground directly in front of her.

"Jolly," she called again and was instantly rewarded when the pup came rushing towards her, wagging her tail profusely, wanting to lick Peta's face. Jumping back in fright, Peta received scratches to her arms and legs as she was entangled in the bushes.

"Good one, Jolly," she remonstrated with the small bundle of fur that seemed to be in the mood to play.

"No, Jolly," Peta told her, putting a note of authority into her voice. She was pleased to see that her command was being listened to, for Jolly sat quietly, looking up into her face. Good, Peta thought.

"Stay," she told her and Jolly obediently laid down, much to her relief.

Now that she had come this far, she thought she might as well see if there was anything inside the cave worth looking at. Excitement and trepidation filled her simultaneously as she crawled the last few paces into the cave's gloomy interior. At first disappointment engulfed her as she looked around thinking she had endured the torture of the last fifteen minutes for nothing, but then something caught her eye and she crawled towards the back of the cave noticing that it was really quite small, being not much bigger than a small room.

A small outcrop of rock jutted out of the cave wall and had been used as a shelf, and Peta stared at a small parcel that looked as if it had been carefully wrapped up to save it from the elements. It was layered with years of dust, but other than this, it appeared to be intact.

Her mind exploded as a thousand thoughts tried to jam themselves into her befuddled brain. Kathleen Jacob's journals! She had stumbled upon Kathleen Jacob's journals; she was sure of it. Everything seemed to fit. The secret hiding place close to the house that had never been found, and most certainly those were her journals sitting there on the rocky outcrop, having been hidden from the outside world for well over a century.

Peta's entire body was shaking as she almost reverently reached for the parcel. When her fingers came into contact with the cloth, she lightly caressed the fabric, finding it slightly rough beneath her fingers. Making herself more comfortable, she sat cross-legged on the floor of the cave, uncaring that she was covering herself with dirt and dust that hadn't been disturbed for many years past. All thoughts of snakes and spiders had long since departed from her mind, which was now fully focused on the thrilling task in front of her, that of opening the journals of Kathleen Isobel Jacobs. Beale's great, great, great grandmother.

She was frustrated beyond belief when she realised she couldn't clearly make out the words written on the pages laid out before her. Not wanting to take the journals away from their secret vault, she carefully wrapped them up again and placed them back on the shelf at the back of the cave. She couldn't wait to get home to tell Beale of her find. Hopefully, he would find them as interesting as she did herself. She looked forward to coming back with him because, together, they could find out the truth about the life of his great, great, great grandmother from journals written by her own hand. She made a mental note to bring a torch next time she visited the cave.

Chapter Seven

THE STATION CAR WAS parked in the driveway at the front of the house when Peta finally returned from her walk. She'd been hoping that Beale would be home and excitedly bounded up the steps, eager to share her find with him.

"Beale!" she called to him excitedly, stopping only long enough to pull her boots off at the front door before striding purposely down the hallway towards their bedroom.

Catching a glimpse of herself in the hallway mirror, she was surprised to see how dishevelled she looked. Small rivulets of congealed blood covered her arms and legs from the scratches she'd sustained on her forced journey through the bushes to the cave entrance. She was covered with dust and grime from head to foot. A small price to pay, she told herself, knowing she would happily endure the discomfort of a few scratches again if the outcome was to be the same.

"Peta, I'm in the drawing room." If her mind hadn't been so fully absorbed on her news, she would have realised that Beale's voice seemed slightly strained.

"Beale, you'll never guess what I f . . . ," Barging into the room at top speed, Peta stopped in her tracks when she saw they had visitors. Beale's mother was looking at her with unconcealed affection, but it was the other person in the room who had captured her attention. Peta's heart had lodged in her throat, and she swallowed convulsively. She was sure she'd paled. The other woman was none other than the blonde woman she had seen Beale escorting when he'd been in Rockhampton. She was looking at Peta with disdain and something else that Peta wasn't able to fathom.

Beale's eyes narrowed slightly when he saw the condition she was in. She had been about to tell him something, but her look of excitement had been replaced by one of expectancy as she looked across at him, waiting to be introduced to their guest.

"What in the name of blazes have you been up to?" he asked more sharply than he had intended. She looked like a street urchin who'd been rolling in the cow pasture, amongst other things. Her arms were covered with bloodied scratches and he thought he could detect a small twig which had entwined itself into the untidy strands of her long hair. It looked unkempt and dirty and full of knots, having come loose from the elastic band she'd used when tying it back from her face.

Peta chose not to answer his query and came fully into the room to stand next to him.

"I'm sorry I didn't know we were expecting visitors." Her clear hazel eyes rested on Beale once more while she waited for him to introduce her. Was it her fault that she looked like something out of the back paddock? If he had warned her, she would have stayed indoors and waited like a dutiful wife for the arrival of their guest.

"Peta," he announced casually, belying a calm he was far from feeling, "this is Marla, an old friend of mine. Marla, this is my wife, Peta. Could I also add that she doesn't normally look like she's in dire need of a hose down."

"Yes, well, I'm sorry about that. Hello, Marla, it's nice to meet you at last. I'm sure you'll forgive me if I don't shake hands. I've been chasing Jolly through the scrub," she lied. She'd have to apologise to Jolly, but she told herself it was only a half lie. She did have to crawl through the bushes to get to her. Never mind that she had stumbled upon the most exciting discovery. She wasn't really sure why she hadn't told them all about her find, but the journals were something she wanted to share with Beale alone. After that, she didn't care who knew. Perhaps it had something to do with the way Marla was looking at her. The other woman was dressed immaculately. Her hair and make-up were done to perfection, and her nails looked to have been professionally manicured. Peta was left in little doubt that those hands had never been digging in the dirt.

Saying a quick hello to Nancy, Peta excused herself, telling them all she wanted to clean herself up and would be right back. Peta had only been in the bedroom a few minutes and was stepping out of her dirt ridden clothes when Beale walked in.

"Peta, are you alright?" He examined the cuts on her arms and could tell at a glance that she didn't get them from chasing Jolly around the property. He would have put his arms around her, but she casually shrugged him away, telling him she was dirty.

"It's never bothered you before when I've been dirty." His words were laced with accuracy and Peta couldn't deny their worth, but she was irked that he hadn't told her of Marla's impending arrival.

"Did you know Marla was coming, Beale?" Peta asked, trying to keep her voice light so as not to arouse his suspicions about the true nature of her query.

"Mum told me the other day that she might be coming for a visit." He didn't add that he had seriously hoped that the proposed visit didn't eventuate. Also, that he'd had grave misgivings about Marla coming to the property. Hopefully, she would see that he and Peta were very happy and leave. He knew marriage had been in Marla's plans, but definitely not in his, at least not to her. Now that he was married to Peta, he hoped she'd leave him alone. She was cloying and annoyed him beyond measure.

"And you didn't think that was a piece of news that should have been passed on to me as your wife," she asked, niggled beyond words that he hadn't told her.

"Peta, don't do this. She's only a friend."

"How good a friend, Beale?" Peta wanted to know as jealousy toward the other woman settled in the pit of her stomach, starting to eat away at her.

The Grazier's Proposal

"Just a friend, nothing else, and even if we had been more to each other, I'm married to you now and might I add I wouldn't change that for the world."

Peta looked up at him, trying to fathom out the information she'd received. The thought that Beale might have been intimate with this other woman didn't bear thinking about. She was still no closer to knowing, and was frustrated beyond measure.

"Hey, you're not jealous, are you?" How could she harbour such a negative emotion when he loved her so dearly?

Choosing not to answer, Peta headed for the bathroom.

"Is that a yes or a no?" he wanted to know as he watched her swagger away. He was sorely tempted to join her. It had been a long day, and he had missed her. He always missed her when he was away from her. He resolved he was going to tell her he loved her and be blowed with the consequences. Surely it could only make things better between them in the long run.

Following her into the bathroom, Beale closed the door behind him and casually leaned against the wall as he watched her strip off the rest of her clothes before turning on the cool jets of water. She had a beautiful, womanly body, full of sexy curves, and he loved to look at her. He could feel his own body responding to her as it always did and damned the people who were waiting for him in the drawing room.

"Where have you really been by the way and don't say chasing Jolly?" he asked, knowing instinctively she hadn't been truthful about her whereabouts.

"Just walking. I fell over a tree trunk," she tacked on for good measure when she saw him looking at her intently. Peta was now reluctant to tell him about her discovery. She felt hurt and disillusioned that she had been the last person to know about Marla's arrival. Had she known, she would have prepared an afternoon tea to welcome the other woman. She had the distinct feeling that Marla didn't approve of her marriage to Beale, but for his sake she would extend the welcome mat out as far as it would go.

"You fell over a tree, I see, and where is this tree exactly?" Beale smilingly quizzed her. He didn't believe her story for a second, and he was curious why she would conceal her true whereabouts from him.

"For heaven's sake, Beale, let it go. Does it really matter?" Peta answered contritely, wanting to be left alone with her thoughts. She didn't want to tell him, but she didn't want to lie to him either, so the best course of action for her to follow was to remain silent.

"Obviously not," came the curt reply. "Don't be long," he tacked on as he walked out of the door.

Peta wanted so desperately to call him back and apologise for her childish behaviour, but her damaged pride forbade her from doing so. Now he was probably angry at her.

"Beale, when are you going to get rid of all of this terribly antiquated furniture and move into the twenty-first century?"

The Grazier's Proposal

Marla had a voice that carried and Peta could hear her quite plainly as she made her way down the hallway towards the drawing room, where she would regretfully have to join the others.

Marla continued, "It's positively depressing. I only wish you'd let me redecorate the last time I was here."

Stepping into the room, Peta said positively, "Lucky for me he didn't let you, Marla. I love the furniture in this house. It would be criminal to remove a single chair." She was showing a bravado that she was far from feeling and was extremely thankful that Beale's mother had agreed to stay for dinner.

Marla's only response was to look down her nose at her before she continued her conversation with Beale.

So it's to be like that, is it, Peta thought. The gloves were off, and Marla was going to fight her.

She looked across at Nancy and was pleased to see the other woman wink at her. "You look very much refreshed, my dear," Nancy told her.

"Yes, it's wonderful what a shower can do for you, isn't it," she smiled back, "but I'm starting to ache all over. I don't think I'm going to be much company tonight, but then I don't think anyone will notice."

The last few words had slipped out and Peta blushed, hating to be caught out in a fit of jealousy. She glanced at Nancy, hoping her words hadn't been heard, but the other woman was looking at her affectionately. She shrugged her shoulders and smiled woefully, feeling instinctively that Nancy understood how she was feeling towards the other woman. I shouldn't have to fight for the attention of my husband, Peta thought as the night wore on. Exhaustion was overpowering her every move, and Peta knew she had to get some sleep. Her body ached and her head had started to throb, a slow monotonous beat that gradually wore her down to the point where she knew she had to make her escape.

Standing up, she swayed slightly as a giddy attack assaulted her and she had to hold on to the arm of her chair to steady herself. Beale was beside her instantly, putting a strong arm around her. She transferred her clammy grasp to him and held on to him, leaning her head against his chest for the next few minutes until the dizziness stopped. She must have gotten a touch of the sun when she'd ventured out today. She hoped that she hadn't been bitten by anything in the cave after all. Perhaps the symptoms she was experiencing were the aftereffects of a spider bite.

When she felt able to speak she said, "I hope you will all excuse me if I leave you to it. I'm sure you both have a lot more catching up to do."

"That's a good idea," Beale agreed, "you look to be all done in." He'd talk to her later about wandering off alone. She had obviously done too much and was exhausted. He didn't plan to be much longer himself. When Beale finally joined her in bed a few hours later, Peta pretended to be asleep. She could smell Marla's cloying perfume on his skin and her eyes filled with unshed tears.

Peta's mood over the next few days slowly disintegrated into a mind sapping depression. Whenever she tried to talk to Beale, he was busy or unavailable, but she noticed that he always seemed to have time for Marla, who never seemed to be far from his side. If he had decided that he wanted the other woman as a life partner, Peta wished he'd have the honesty to say so. That way she could gather what was left of her shredded dignity and leave.

At first, Peta had tried to extend the hand of friendship to Marla, but it was evident that the other woman wasn't the least bit interested in cultivating a friendship with her. The only time she was courteous to Peta was of an evening when Beale was around. Other than this, Peta was ignored and if she was to be truthful, she had to admit she preferred Marla's lack of friendliness because this meant that she didn't have to play the part of the willing hostess. She was stunned when Beale attacked her about her lack of manners regarding Marla.

"Is this some sort of a joke?" she shot back at him, thoroughly sick of the waspish verbal assaults she'd had to endure from their guest over the course of the last few days. Beale's censure was the last straw, and Peta's frayed nerves finally exploded in a fiery burst of temper.

"The woman's a viper, but she's very careful when it comes to hiding her true feelings from you. I have tried to be friendly towards her, but your little friend has thrown all of my efforts back in my face. If she's told you anything else, she's lying."

Upon delivering this heated message, Peta stormed out of the room, uncaring of the trouble her caustic words would cause in the household. To be perfectly frank, Peta thought belatedly, that was a lie. If Beale knew how she felt, perhaps he'd ask Marla to leave. She couldn't understand why he'd let the visit drag on for so long anyway, unless he actually liked having that awful woman around. Although she would have bet everything she owned, Marla wasn't the type of woman he'd be attracted to.

Marla's presence in the house had changed the way Peta and Beale responded to each other. Their relationship was courteous, but strained. Gone were the intimate interludes they'd shared, along with the heated kisses and caresses they'd lavished upon each other when their needs had overwhelmed them. Although they shared a bed, that was where the intimacy stopped. Peta ached for Beale, but she wasn't going to beg her husband to love her.

Peta thought her suspicions had to be correct. Why, just today, she'd seen Beale smiling at Marla regarding something she'd said. It tore at Peta's heart to see them together. She gets the welcome mat and I get the drawn shutters, she thought sadly to herself.

Each day she managed to slip away to the cave and once there she would lose herself in another world, finding solace in the journals of Kathleen Jacobs. If she was missed, nobody mentioned it to her. Nancy had been called away to the coast where her sister was sick, and Peta felt she had lost her one true ally when her mother-in-law left.

How Peta wished she had someone that she could talk her problems over with. Her heart felt bruised and slightly battered, making her feel that she had the weight of the whole world on her shoulders.

Her thoughts immediately turned to Nelson, who was probably her best friend in the entire world. He always knew how to make her smile, even when she was in the midst of a deepest depression. He had the knack of knowing how to make her laugh at herself, but she was sure that even he couldn't bring a smile to her lips this time.

Her mind involuntarily returned to the scene she had witnessed between Marla and Beale the night before. Peta had been in the kitchen putting the finishing touches to their meal, while Beale and Marla had been in the games room playing pool. Peta could hear Marla's incessant chatter, and usually she could block it out. The other woman's voice annoyed her to distraction.

Marla was trying to press a point with Beale, and Peta shook with suppressed anger as she stood listening. She wondered just how far Marla would go and then wondered just how far Beale would let her go before he asked her to stop.

"Face facts, Beale, she doesn't even acknowledge that you're in the room most of the time. How much more evidence do you need? For heaven's sake, wake up to yourself. How can someone be so astute at the business of running a cattle station, but when it comes to the business of the heart, be so stupid? It's not too late, darling, if you would only tell her you've realised that you've made a terrible mistake in marrying her. Marrying on the rebound is something that can always be fixed."

Peta took in every painful word. She wondered if perhaps Marla had meant for her to hear those hateful words. The other woman was finally throwing down the gauntlet. Until now her jibes had been cruel, but this outburst was laced with pure venom and it was meant to kill any feelings that Beale might have for Peta. It was up to Peta to see that this hateful woman's taunts weren't taken seriously, but for the life of her, she didn't know what to do. It was true that she hadn't told Beale in so many words that she loved him, but surely he knew how happy he made her. Surely he realised that! He took her to paradise every time they made love, but he had never told her he loved her either, so how could she declare her love for him. Suddenly, life had become very complicated.

How could she not be aware of him? His presence was everywhere. The shoes left casually at the back door; the shirt thrown across the back of the chair, the fragrant scent of his aftershave which filled the very air she breathed. Oh, how could she not be aware of him? She was totally aware of him as her husband and as a man. His touch, even the most casual, brought her completely undone. She yearned for him, pined for him . . . loved him.

Peta couldn't delay going back into the other room any longer, although she doubted that her presence had been missed.

The sight that greeted her as she walked into the games room made her physically sick. Beale and Marla were embracing, in fact they were kissing. Peta could feel the colour drain out from her face as she witnessed the hateful scene. She must have gasped, for Beale spun around to face her. He looked pale beneath his tan, while Marla's face was covered in victory.

"It's not what you think, Peta," Beale tried to explain as he stepped away from the other woman.

"No, of course it isn't. It never is," she answered him, proud of herself that her voice sounded completely normal to her ears. She quickly turned on her heel, retreating back the way she'd come, and fled from the house out into the gathering darkness.

Peta felt numb! She wasn't aware of how long she sat staring into the nothingness of space. She had been totally stripped of all feeling and felt hollow inside. What did she do now? Did she calmly go back inside and face them, telling them she hoped they'd be happy, but would they mind if she stayed till morning or whenever. Would Beale try to find her? She really didn't know. Would finding her be his last act of chivalry towards her before he bade her goodbye?

Deciding she would save him the effort, knowing instinctively that she wasn't ready to face either one of them, she made her way carefully towards the office outbuildings hoping she'd be able to spend the night on one of the couches in Vic's office.

"What in blazes . . . , Missus, is that you? Now what are you doing down here at this time of night?" Vic had been about ready to turn in when he'd heard a noise in the office and had come to investigate. One look at Peta's pale face and shock ridden eyes had been enough to tell him that there was trouble up at the main house and he didn't need a crystal ball to tell him who was behind all the mischief.

Vic knew instinctively when he'd seen Marla, that she would cause trouble. He couldn't understand how Beale couldn't see through her, nor could he understand why he'd let her set foot on the place after the last time. The men all thought they had seen the last of her, and good riddance, with her high and mighty airs and graces when Beale brought Peta home as his wife. She was like a breath of fresh air, that one. There wasn't a man on the place who didn't have a soft spot in his heart for the new missus. In the short time she'd been here, she had successfully won over every man on the place just by being her sweet natural self.

"I need somewhere to sleep, Vic," Peta told him quietly, not wanting to elaborate on the cause of the trouble. When she was gone, Beale still had to live and work with these men. It was better if they didn't know the circumstances which surrounded her flight from the house.

Vic was kindness itself as he prepared a bed for her in the spare room next to his office. He mostly remained silent, but he insisted she drink the cup of tea that he made for her. He had liberally laced it with rum, telling her it would help her sleep, and indeed it did.

Once Peta was asleep, Vic went into the office and rang through to the main house. He didn't feel he was letting Peta down by letting Beale know the whereabouts of his wife. The way he saw it, Beale would come and wake him anyway if he thought he needed to start a search and he was duty bound to tell his boss where his wife was sleeping.

Beale answered almost immediately. His voice sounded strained and Vic could detect concern mixed with a bone weariness that, he realised, had nothing to do with tiredness.

Peta's dreams were full of strange shadows and whisperings and she muttered sadly to herself, trying to dispel the overpowering presence of Beale because he no longer belonged to her, but he wouldn't go away. She cried out to him in her dream, wanting him, while wet tears flowed unchecked down her pale cheeks.

A strong hand gently wiped them away while a soft, tender voice whispered lovingly to her, supplying her with the comfort she so badly craved. She took comfort from that voice because it was telling her how very much she was loved. She smiled tentatively, wanting to believe the voice as it kept repeating over and over that she was loved. Her hand was enveloped and held securely, and it was only then that she was able to drift into a deep, soundless sleep where her dreams were peaceful and calming.

"Peta," Vic called her quietly intruding into her troubled thoughts, "The boys and I are going to take you swimming so go and get your gear. There's a good girl."

"What?" she was sitting in the men's mess hall nursing a half-empty cup of tea. If anyone wondered why she was there, she wasn't challenged about it. The men would need to be deaf and blind if they didn't know what had been going on for the last few days up at the main house.

"I said get your swimming gear the boys and I are taking you out for the day to see the sights." His voice was commanding, but Peta could detect an undertone of kindness belying the request.

She knew the men were as confused as she was herself at the recent turn of events since Marla's arrival at the homestead.

"I can't," she stated forlornly, looking up into the older man's face, knowing he knew the reason she was refusing to go up to the main house.

"They're not there, Peta," he told her quietly. "Beale asked me to tell you he was going into town. He'll be back later on today. We figure if he can have a day off, so can we."

"Oh," Peta replied, a little sadly to the information she'd been given. So Beale and Marla had gone off together. He didn't even have the decency to tell me himself, she thought.

Despite her wounded heart, Peta had a wonderful day with the men. They gave her a marvellous time, showing her some of the scenery that made up Blackrock Downs, but the most spectacular by far had to be Deadman's Gorge.

"I don't believe it!" Peta was enthralled by the view that was spread out before her. Deadman's Gorge started out as nothing more than a deep gully, but as you travelled further up the narrow ravine, it opened out into a vast valley that was flanked on either side by steep mountain ranges.

A natural spring bubbled up out of the rocks, then cascaded serenely down the sides of a rocky outcrop, and it was this that formed the large pool of water that was spread out so majestically before them. The pool must be bottomless because the water didn't go anywhere; there wasn't a river or a creek that derived its humble beginnings from the pool. Mother Nature in her infinite wisdom had created a lifeline for any weary travellers who happened to come this way, for it was the only water for miles around according to Vic.

"It's something, isn't it," Vic said, standing by her side. "This is where Blackrock gets its water supply. I would have thought Beale would have brought you out here himself."

"We were supposed to come here on our way home after the wedding, but we stayed in Rockhampton instead," she told him, trying to stop the wobble that had appeared in her voice at the mention of Beale and their wedding. To her dismay, hot tears scalded her eyes, blurring the beautiful view that was laid out before her.

Peta swiped at them angrily, not wanting tears to spoil this day, determined she wasn't going to feel sorry for herself. She had taken a gamble on Beale falling in love with her, and she had lost. It was as simple as that. She should be thankful that he realised his mistake early in their marriage. She was strong and in time she would get over her love for Beale. Who knows, maybe she would even fall in love again, but her heart lurched painfully at the thought of walking away from the one man she had ever truly loved.

He'd have to make some decisions as to the terms of their marriage, but she supposed his love for Marla had won out in the end. She hoped he wouldn't lose Blackrock because there was no way the terms of his father's will could now be fulfilled. He had run out of time and options. His love for the other woman must be very strong if he was willing to give up everything for her. She wondered if Marla would still appreciate Beale if he had nothing to offer her. She hoped the attraction the other woman had for Beale was based on love and not just on material gain. She didn't want him to be hurt.

"Come on, Peta, get your hands dirty. Come and tell us what you want here." The boys had taken her to a natural clay pan and were digging out great clumps of clay from which they said she could sculpt a great masterpiece.

Peta didn't have the heart to tell them that the clay was next to useless for the kind of sculpture they had in mind, so in she went, boots and all.

She was dropped off at her doorstep late in the afternoon and trudged up the front steps, wearily waving a last goodbye to the men as they made their way back down to their quarters. She threw them a kiss for good measure. A lovely long soak in the bath was going to be her first priority. She would never forget their kindness to her. It warmed her heart to think of the seven men she had spent the day with. They hadn't allowed her to be sad and had filled every minute of her day with adventure, not giving her the time to think about her relationship with Beale, nor had they questioned her about why she had spent the night in Vic's spare room.

A movement caught her eye as she neared the top of the steps and she involuntarily stiffened, expecting to see Beale framed in the doorway. She wasn't ready to confront him on the matter of his inexplicable behaviour with Marla.

"Nelson?" she said, completely baffled by her friend's appearance at the property. She stood transfixed to the spot, totally dumbstruck, and then let out a yell of pure joy as she raced up the rest of the steps to throw herself into the arms of her friend.

"Nelson, oh, Nelson, it's so good to see you. Is it really you?" she sobbed, overcome by spontaneous emotion. Nelson was here. How, or why, didn't seem to be important. She had needed him, and miraculously he had arrived.

"Jupiter?" Nelson was just as stunned by her unexpected appearance at the property. He lifted her chin up with one of his long fingers and gazed into her hazel eyes. He perceived correctly that something was wrong, and he'd get to the bottom of the problem in due course, but for now he wanted to know about the chain of events that had brought her out to his friend's property.

"What a sight for sore eyes," he continued, then added, "What brings you out to this godforsaken place? Talk about heavenly bodies appearing out of the blue." He had arrived about half an hour ago to a deserted homestead, so had come in and made himself at home as he always did. He presumed Beale was out riding the range somewhere and would eventually make an appearance at the end of the day. If he was further afield, he would leave him a note, stay the night, and be on his way first thing in the morning, as was his custom when he arrived unannounced at the property.

"Nelson, please don't call me Jupiter. You know how much I hate it." To her consternation she started to cry and was powerless to stop the flow of tears as they coursed unchecked down her pale cheeks.

"Okay, if you feel that strongly about it," Nelson joked, jumping in with a quip that was meant to break the tension he could feel building up within her.

Peta lifted watery eyes up to him and smiled feebly. She was so glad to see him and had so much to tell him. They had moved inside and were sitting in the drawing room. Nelson continued questioning Peta about her presence at the property.

"How do you know Beale, Jupiter?" he wanted to know.

Taking a deep breath to calm herself, she told him simply, "Beale and I are married, Nelson."

"No!" Nelson exclaimed, looking down into her face. "When did all of this happen? The last time I saw you, you were bemoaning the fact that you couldn't find anyone worth taking a second look at, and now you're trying to tell me you're married to my best bud!"

"Your best bud!" Peta echoed. "Since when? I've never heard you talk about Beale before."

"Rubbish. Remember the last time I was in town I couldn't go to the movies with you because I had to meet someone?" at her nod of remembrance he said, "That was Beale. We're old mates from way back. My company has been supplying Blackrock Downs with their equipment for years, but let's get to the interesting stuff like how in blazes you two met and more importantly why wasn't I invited to the wedding."

Peta entertained the notion of lying to her friend about the circumstances of her wedding to Beale, but she found she couldn't bring herself to go through with it. She wasn't a person who lied easily so as delicately as she could, she explained to him why she had married Beale leaving nothing out.

Nelson had remained silent, listening attentively while Peta poured out her heart to him. "I see," he said at last, "so where is he now?"

Shrugging her slim shoulders, Peta told him she didn't know. All she knew was that Beale and Marla had left the homestead together sometime this morning.

Looking at Peta intently, Nelson said, "Beale is not the kind of man who would marry someone and then run off with an old flame. If he committed himself to you, regardless of the reason, then he will honour that commitment, Jupiter. If you believe nothing else that I've said, believe that!"

"Why couldn't you have arrived a week ago when I really needed you," she wanted to know, flinging herself across the settee into his arms where she was enveloped in a great bear hug.

"Am I interrupting anything," Beale's voice alerted them to the fact that he'd arrived home.

"No," Nelson told him casually, looking over the top of Peta's head towards the door where Beale was standing, "I'm just catching up on all the news about your recent wedding from your lovely wife here." Nelson wouldn't let her go, and Peta was forced to turn around stiffly in his arms to look at her husband. His mouth was set rigidly in an uncompromising line, making Peta realise explanations were called for.

"Nelson," she squirmed uncomfortably, "will you please let me go. Beale is going to get the wrong impression."

To Beale she said, "Would you believe I know this big galute? We are, in fact, very good friends."

"Pleased to hear it," Beale answered her, coming fully into the room. He was reeling from the shock of seeing his wife happily ensconced in the arms of his best friend. He was also dead tired, having driven for most of the day, wanting to have Marla off the property and deposited at the nearest airport. After last night's fiasco, he'd told her to get off the property and not to return. Now all he wanted was to set matters straight with Peta.

"I was pleased to hear that you'd finally met your match, Beale, and about time, too. Do you know I had a thing for Jupiter, but she turned me down flat years ago? Your powers of persuasion must be very intense. We lived together for a while, but it didn't work out, I found her to be too bossy."

Peta was looking at Nelson as if he'd lost his mind. Why was he carrying on like this? Not a word of truth had just come out of his mouth. "Nelson, that's the biggest load of rubbish I ever heard. I stayed with you and Helen, not lived with you when my grandmother passed away before I moved to Rockhampton."

"What's the difference," he asked innocently, "stayed, lived, it's the same thing."

She implored him with her eyes to stop this stupid charade. The last thing she wanted was to alienate Beale any further than he already seemed to be. She was certainly going to have a piece of Nelson when she finally had him to herself again.

"Beale doesn't want to listen to your silly banter, so will you kindly shut up," Peta told him as she wiggled out of his embrace.

"On the contrary, I find it most interesting, but I'm afraid it will have to wait for another time. I can see that I'm leaving Peta in capable hands, Nelson. I'm sure I'll see you both later." After delivering this curt retort, Beale turned on his heel and swiftly walked out of the room.

Nelson turned to Peta to enquire innocently, "Do you think it was something I said?"

"Always the clown, aren't you, Nelson!"

"If I'm so funny, why aren't you laughing?"

Peta looked up into the face of her friend and sent him a lop-sided grin, although her hazel eyes remained sad. "If I asked you especially nicely to butt out of my business and leave well enough alone, would you do it?"

She was given a skeptical look for her trouble, followed by, "Now you know me better than that. When have I ever been able to mind my own business?"

"Never to my recollection," she whispered feebly, already sorry that she had opened her heart to him about her troubles with Beale.

"There's your answer then," he responded.

"You are to do nothing, Nelson, do you understand? . . . Nothing! I'm not sixteen anymore and I don't need any heads bashed in, metaphorically or otherwise," Peta could see that the wheels of his devious mind were starting to turn and knowing what he was capable of doing, she quickly repeated herself, tapping her index finger on his forehead, "Nothing, nothing, nothing. You are to stay completely out of this. I'll work it out for myself."

"Absolutely, anything you say, but is it alright if I talk to my friend while I'm here? Does that meet with your approval?"

"I mean it, Nelson, stay out of it," Peta told him yet again, "you've caused enough trouble for one day, my friend, and you've only been here two minutes so quit while you're ahead." She gave him a quick punch on his shoulder to drive home her point.

"Ow, that hurt," he told her, then added laughingly as he rubbed his shoulder, "you hit like a girl."

Already Nelson's devious mind was thinking up ways to force Beale into admitting that he was in love with his wife. He hadn't missed the thunderous expression on Beale's face when he'd walked into the room and had seen Peta being affectionately held in another man's arms.

Peta was up bright and early the next morning. Having Nelson here had cheered her immensely, and she couldn't wait to see him. There was so much that she wanted to ask him about their mutual friends in Brisbane. She realised how out of touch she'd become and remorsefully promised herself that she would sit down and write to each and every one of them before the week was out.

She hadn't expected to find Beale still in the homestead and was therefore surprised when she ran into him in the kitchen. He was feeding the scraps of his breakfast to Jolly, who was becoming quite adept at scavenging food from the kitchen.

"Oh," she said, "I thought Nelson was in here." She couldn't believe how stilted they'd become in each other's presence. When she had finally gone to bed last night, he'd been lying on his back staring at the ceiling, but when she had walked into the bedroom, he turned onto his side, effectively ignoring her.

He's wishing I was Marla, she told herself as she covertly watched him fondling Jolly's ears.

Beale glanced up from patting Jolly on the head and the little dog jumped up, resting her front paws on his leg, not wanting him to stop petting her.

"He went down to see Vic," Beale told her, using an economy of words. Peta could see that he was definitely out of sorts this morning and as such, was someone to be avoided. Perhaps later, when he was calmer, they could talk about her close friendship with Nelson, because that was all it was, a friendship.

"Oh." Peta's disappointment was unmistakable, and Beale looked at her intently.

"What's the 'Oh' for?" he wanted to know. His words were liberally laced with sarcasm.

"Meaning?" Peta asked evenly, not wanting to be drawn into an argument with him.

"I think you know exactly what I mean," Beale replied, looking at her unflinchingly. He held her hazel orbs captive, not giving her the luxury of being able to look away.

"Quite frankly, I don't, so why don't you tell me," she threw back at him spiritedly, feeling her anger rising. She was sure she wasn't going to like whatever it was Beale was going to say.

Beale stared intently at her from across the room, and it seemed to Peta that he was weighing up the pros and cons of the impact his words might have on her.

He said, "While it's not part of our agreement that you should love me, I would appreciate it very much if you'd restrain yourself from flirting with every man who happens to cross your path. As my wife, you have a certain standard to maintain."

"A certain standard to maintain!" Peta was incredulous and furiously angry. She exploded, asking him heatedly, "What about your standards, Beale? It seems to me that your behaviour with Marla would fall into the category of a flirtatious dalliance, wouldn't you say, or does your prestigious position as owner of Blackrock Downs give you an exemption?"

Having flung these words at him, she turned and walked sedately out of the room with her head held high. Not for a second would she let him see how much his hateful accusations had hurt her. Please don't let him follow me, she prayed silently, for she knew if he was to confront her again, her fragile facade would crumble.

Chapter Eight

"I MADE ONE STUPID mistake, Nelson. I fell in love and now I'm miserable. Beale doesn't love me. I don't think he even likes me very much anymore. I wish I'd never agreed to this stupid marriage." Peta looked up into the face of her friend, expecting to see compassion etched into the fine lines that feathered out from his normally sympathetic brow.

Instead, she was surprised to see his eyes were dancing crystals, flashing with barely controlled amusement.

"Balderdash! I've never seen anyone so smitten. The man's besotted with you. The trouble is you're both too stubborn to admit it to each other. Do you want to know something else? He's as jealous as hell." Seeing the unbelieving look Peta cast in his direction, he continued, "He is . . . of me and probably any man who even looks like showing a sexual interest in you."

"That's absolutely ridiculous," Peta stammered, wanting so much to credit Beale with loving her, "I wish I could believe you."

Since their heated words this morning, Peta had been miserable. It wouldn't do to let herself think Beale could ever return her love.

"Now what can I do to convince you I'm right," Nelson regarded her shrewdly with a thoughtful expression covering his face.

Beale had been closeted in his office with the door closed for the last few hours. He was supposed to be writing up a story that he'd promised to do for a cattle journal on the benefits of hand feeding during times of drought, but the words kept dancing around the page and he wasn't able to concentrate. In a moment of pure frustration, he viciously hurled the pen he'd been holding across the room, shattering it into tiny fragments as it forcibly hit the wall.

His mind kept wandering back to Peta and the lousy accusation he'd flung at her. His foul mood hadn't improved over the course of the day, and the last person he'd wanted to see walk casually into his office was Nelson.

Nelson had spent the better part of the day trying to dissuade Peta from packing up her belongings and leaving with him when he left in the morning.

"Is this where you've been hiding yourself? I've been looking for you. Do you fancy a game of pool before dinner? Peta's cooking a roast and she tells me it won't be ready for a while yet, so there's plenty of time for me to beat you in a game or two while I work up an appetite." Nelson asked nonchalantly. The other man's face looked drawn and strained.

"Sorry, Nelson," Beale answered shortly, "but I have other priorities at the moment. Business before pleasure and all that. These books need some tender loving care if I'm ever going to get them to balance." He had long since given up on trying to write a story for the god damn magazine.

Nelson perched himself on the corner of Beale's office desk, thinking to himself that the time to have that fatherly talk with Beale had arrived. He'd had enough, and the time for action was now.

"Tell me," he asked abrasively, "is there any tender loving care up there with those priorities when it comes to Jupiter?"

Beale looked up into the face of his friend, wanting to know if there was an ulterior motive behind the probing question. It was certainly the first time in their long friendship that he could remember Nelson being anything but positive and friendly, but then he reasoned the stakes were very high. He thought it was fairly obvious that Nelson was referring to the heated words he'd had with Peta this morning.

"Why?" he shot back caustically, thinking with an increasing hostility that it was no one's business but his own the way he spoke to his wife.

"Why?" Nelson repeated, thoroughly fed up with this blockhead of a man who sat so defiantly before him. Beale's hands were rigidly holding a fountain pen, and Nelson detected the increasing pressure that was being placed on the instrument. "Why," he repeated yet again, "because you stupid blockhead the demented woman loves you. Personally, I can't see why, but I guess there's no accounting for taste. She always did have lousy taste when it came to picking out her men."

He could see his outburst had produced the desired effect on Beale, who looked as if he'd been hit by a train. Nelson had the satisfaction of seeing him pale beneath his healthy tan. This was definitely a good sign. Now we're getting somewhere, he thought.

Beale ran shaking fingers through his thick stock of jet black hair before he looked back at his friend, wanting conformation. "Did she tell you that?"

"Not exactly," Nelson wasn't ready to divulge this bit of information just yet, "but you don't have to be a brain surgeon to figure it out. Kind of makes you feel pretty stupid, hey," Nelson told him, thoroughly enjoying this superiority he had over Beale at the moment. He continued, "So I take it this means you care for her in some small measure then?"

The tormented look Beale directed at him was laced with pure malice and he longed to make a derogatory remark about his friend's parentage, but he held his tongue, saying instead, "Some small measure, yes. Nelson, I love her so much it's tearing me apart. I thought I'd lost her to you and I wanted to kill you!"

"Ouch, I'm glad we got that small error cleared up," Nelson smiled across at Beale. He was glad he'd forced the issue. Now perhaps things will get back to normal around here. He added in a more businesslike manner, "Okay, so what are you going to do about it?"

Beale smiled ruefully. "I don't know. You say you don't really know if she loves me. Do you have any suggestions tucked away anywhere?"

The Grazier's Proposal

"You really are a blockhead, aren't you?"

"Do you have to keep calling me that? It's really starting to get on my nerves," Nelson was told irritably.

"If the shoe fits, my friend," Nelson threw at him, totally unperturbed by Beale's threatening manner.

Nelson was well pleased with the way his meddling had turned out. Now, if he could just see Peta and have another talk with her, he surmised his work here would be finished.

His opportunity came sooner than he expected, for it was during dinner that Crawfish came bounding up the front stairs and knocked loudly on the door before walking in. He smiled a grim greeting at them all and then launched into the reason why he was here.

"Boss, there's been a flash flood up in the hills and the water's coming down the gully fairly fast. We're going to have to move the cattle we brought in yesterday. Vic said if we wait any longer we run the risk of losing them. He also said to tell you it's going to mean all hands on deck because of the team you sent to muster in the scrub."

Beale didn't need this distraction. He had wanted to talk to Peta, to set things straight between them, for if Nelson was correct in his assumption that she loved him, then it was high time she knew the truth about his all-consuming love for her. Perhaps there was a chance for them after all.

"Do you want me to come out with you, Beale?" Nelson offered his limited services, although he knew he'd be next to useless out on the run.

"Thanks, but no. Actually I'd appreciate it if you stayed here with Peta."

Beale was already out of his chair and was moving towards the door when he doubled back and walked over to where Peta was sitting, toying with her food. "When I get back, Peta, I think we should talk. There are some details that I think have to be straightened out between us."

He glanced across at Nelson, thinking he'd see a look of pious satisfaction plastered on his friend's face, but instead, Nelson was puckering up, telling him with his actions that he should give her a kiss. Damn it, wasn't the man ever serious, Beale thought as he stared incredulously at his friend. There were times when he wondered about Nelson's sanity, and this occasion definitely had to be one of them. He'd kiss his wife later in the privacy of their bedroom. There he'd tell her how much she meant to him. He knew if he was to start kissing her now, he wouldn't want to leave.

He gave Nelson a searching look, trying to decide if he could be entrusted with his wife's welfare. What if he'd been lying about Peta loving him and they were planning to leave together? He realised he had to trust his instincts, and they told him to fight for the woman he loved more than life itself.

Nelson sat silently for a moment, then faced Peta squarely. He told her candidly, "You know what the problem is, don't you?"

At her look of pure ignorance, he raised his eyebrows, expecting her to realise that the solution to her problem was right in front of her.

"Oh, for heaven's sake!" he admonished her severely. "You have to tell him you love him. Don't you see! You love each other . . . no, hear me out," he told her putting up a hand to silence her when she would have interrupted him, then he continued, saying again, "You love each other, but the way the situation stands at the moment neither one of you will take the initiative and blurt it out. There can be no trust where there is no commitment, Jupiter."

"But I am committed to this marriage," she wailed at him.

"Beale doesn't know that. He knows you are compatible, yes, but that isn't love. Why do you think he's so distant towards you at the moment?"

"Because of Marla. He has feelings for her," she told him, keeping her voice neutral.

"See what I mean." he pointed a finger at her, making her smile feebly despite herself. Nelson could be very melodramatic when he was trying to make a point. He continued, "Trust is the key, Jupiter. If the silly blockhead knew you loved him, and heard it from your own lips, he'd trust you, but as things stand . . . ," he deliberately let his voice trail off, hoping his words would have the desired effect.

He continued, thoroughly enjoying the role he was playing. "In effect, his silence is telling the world, see if I care that my beautiful, sexy wife is paying way too much attention to another man, but let me tell you, Jupiter, the blockhead is hurting like hell. He won't admit it. He has too much pride, and he's not entirely sure of you. Love wasn't a part of your marriage bargain so he's playing it tough, but you mark my words every time some unattached male has the misfortune to walk onto Blackrock Downs, Beale's jealousy is going to rise to the surface."

"But I'm not paying too much attention to you!" Peta exclaimed, shocked into answering, "I've only been talking to you."

"Exactly!" he agreed sweetly.

"Oh . . . ," she bit her lip, "but he can't be jealous of you."

"And why not!" came the indignant reply.

"Damn it, Nelson! Cut it out. You know what I mean." His smile told her he knew exactly what she meant.

"If you're correct," she said, daring to smile as the unsaid words filled her heart, "that means he loves me." The tears came then, and Peta threw herself into Nelson's arms, sobbing uncontrollably. Perhaps there was hope for her marriage, after all.

The sound of Beale's footsteps made her pull quickly away from the shelter of Nelson's arms. She didn't want him to gain the wrong impression yet again about why she was in Nelson's arms, but she wasn't quick enough and Beale observed the innocent embrace.

"Beale," Nelson said casually to his friend. His arm was still thrown informally around Peta's shoulder. "We thought you'd be gone for most of the night. Did you forget something?"

Peta lifted tear-stained eyes to her husband. She could detect a small pulse hammering along his strong jawline, and knew instantly that he was upset by the scene he thought he'd interrupted. It was evident that he'd drawn the incorrect conclusion and she could have kicked

Nelson, who was making matters worse with his cavalier attitude towards her.

"Is there something I can do for you, Beale?" she asked him, but even to her own ears the words sounded hollow and meaningless, as if they'd been uttered in a moment of panic.

Beale looked down at her through eyes that were devoid of any emotion. "No, nothing." His words were clipped and precise, having been delivered with a cool courtesy.

Peta watched miserably as he walked away. Seconds later, she heard the roar of the station car that told her he was gone. As long as she lived, she would never understand the complexities that went into making up the heart and soul of the male animal known as man.

"You have to tell him, Jupiter," Nelson told her simply.

"When did you get to be so wise?" she wanted to know.

"Years of meddling in other people's business," he said, trying to bring a light touch back into the conversation.

Peta stood forlornly on the front verandah, watching Nelson's car grow smaller on the horizon as he drove off into the distance. Beale wasn't back from the muster and an endless day stretched out in front of her where she would only have herself for company. Usually this was enough for her, but today she didn't feel like doing any of the usual things that made up her busy schedule. A thought struck her, and she eagerly made her way to the kitchen, where she pulled her knapsack off the peg behind the door and started stuffing it with food and water.

She had decided she would spend the day at the cave, where she would read some more of Kathleen Jacob's journals. Peta found the journals intriguing and wondered yet again how this woman had escaped death at the hands of a drunken husband.

"Okay, Jolly, I think this will do us. We have enough food to feed an army." Bending down, she fondled the dog's ears, then headed for the door, telling Jolly to follow her. Peta automatically grabbed her hat from the peg behind the back door and placed it jauntily onto her head. She felt a certain pride which she knew was utterly ridiculous every time she placed the Akubra on her head, but she felt the symbolism that the Australian icon placed on her made her feel more at home in these unfamiliar surroundings. It made her look the part, therefore she was the part.

Arriving at her destination a short time later, Peta poured herself a cup of tea from the flask she'd brought with her. She sat on one of the rocks that made up the entrance to the cave and surveyed the surrounding countryside. To the untrained eye it looked desolate and barren, devoid of all life, but Peta was starting to appreciate the raw, naked beauty that the outback offered.

"Beautiful," she breathed in the dry air, appreciating, as an artist, the spectacular spectrum of colours which could be seen everywhere one cared to look. "What a wonderful painting this would make."

Peta was amazed at how well preserved the journals were. Still, she unwrapped them with infinite care, not wanting to risk damaging a single page. She presumed the hot dry weather had a lot to do with their perfect condition.

Peta was completely fascinated by the writings of the other woman. Her heart went out to Kathleen as she read of the hardships this poor woman had endured at the hands of an uncaring, drunken husband. Battling the harsh elements would have been difficult enough, Peta thought, for Mother Nature could turn on you at any time, but she would also have had to conquer her fears. The fear of death was uppermost in her mind, because if she was to die, who would raise her child.

A child! So there had been a child born to her first husband. Interesting, Peta thought, as she scanned the pages of an earlier journal looking for evidence of a birth and was rewarded when she came across details which confirmed the birth of a son.

Peta read page after page, becoming fully absorbed in the life of Beale's great, great, great grandmother. Towards the end of the last journal, she had written that her husband had become sick. She had tried to nurse him, but to no avail. He simply went to sleep one night and failed to wake up.

It amazed Peta to think of the heartfelt relief she felt as she read that particular entry in the other woman's journal. Kathleen had been freed from a heavy yoke which had been placed around her neck, weighing her down. There was also a sense of freedom to finally live her life, which was now free from oppression.

Almost instantly the journals became light-hearted and full of the joy of living. Kathleen wrote of hope, telling of a new love and anticipated happiness.

One particular entry pulled at Peta's heart. It was a love letter addressed to the man whom Kathleen had married after the death of her first husband. Peta read, feeling as if she was violating this woman's innermost thoughts, but she was powerless to stop herself.

To my own true love, my beloved husband, Beale.

How I have loved you over the years. I have been rewarded by you in kind, for your love for me has been my protection, my haven, and my greatest comfort. You delivered me from the gates of Hades where I lay crushed and broken, giving me a reason to dare to live again. From the first moment I saw you, I knew I was doomed to love you for eternity.

The years have passed far too swiftly, and we have grown old together, my love, but now the time has arrived when I must leave you for I can hear my name being whispered by the wind which blows ever so gently over me as I lay here in our bed waiting for death to finally claim me. Take comfort in the knowledge that I have loved you with all of my heart and soul. I will take this love with me to the grave and hand it back to you when we meet again on the other side.

Be brave, my beloved, and know that I love you.

Forever yours, Kathleen.

The Grazier's Proposal

When Peta had finally finished reading, she couldn't hold back the flow of tears that fell unchecked down her cheeks. This brave woman's strength was somehow reaching out to touch her, daring her to fight for her own husband's love and for their marriage.

Kathleen didn't elaborate on how her second husband had come into her life, only that he had. Peta found this to be strange when she had catalogued everything else so carefully.

Searching through the journals for information about Kathleen's second husband, Peta was overjoyed when she found another two letters. The first must have been written soon after Kathleen's marriage to her Beale.

The feeling that she was trespassing on very private feelings wouldn't go away, but Peta couldn't put the journals down. Something inside her was compelling her to read on. She read …

To my beloved,

Together, in my secret hiding place, you helped me to chase away the ghosts of my past. You laid with me, holding me close as only a lover can until the fear was gone. I was swept away by my need for you and all that remained after that sweet moment was precious memories where once there was only fear.

You filled my heart with wonderment and a sweet longing which I had not known before. Anticipation has replaced the fear driving this hated emotion away. Now my hiding place is a secret no longer, my love, because eagerly I share it with you, only with you.

All my love, Kathleen.

Peta's throat was constricted with pent up emotion. She couldn't help but feel happy for this woman who'd had to bear so much pain and suffering. With trembling fingers, she lifted the second letter to the light and started to read.

Kathleen has gone. She left me this morning in the early hours. She has taken my heart with her and now I am an empty shell, impatiently waiting for the time when I can be with her again. Only then will my longing for her be assuaged. Kathleen assures me we will meet again and my heart believes that we will. These past forty-two years with Kathleen as my wife have been the happiest of my life.

Sleep peacefully, my beloved, and dream of me.

Forever yours, Beale.

Peta's heart broke as she read these words. There was such a poignant sadness to them. Their love had been so enduring, so strong and passionate that Peta didn't think death would separate them. Tears flooded her eyes as she gave in to the melancholy that totally engulfed her. Jolly looked up at her questioningly, not understanding what was wrong, and Peta pulled the dog onto her lap and cried into her soft fur. Great heart wrenching sobs were torn from her body, exhausting her completely.

If Peta was to analyse her behaviour, she would have realised that her tears were also for herself and the unhappy situation she found herself in.

Waking with a start, Peta realised she must have fallen asleep. She wondered momentarily where she was then as realisation dawned on her, so did the time.

"Oh, hell!" She exclaimed as she looked at her watch then frantically gathered up the contents of her knapsack, "Beale will be home and wondering where the heck I am." She looked across at Jolly asking her crossly, "Why didn't you wake me up." The little dog responded to the scolding by crawling across to her on her belly and licked her dutifully on the arm. Peta relented, "It's alright, Jolly, I was only joking."

Having arrived back at the homestead around midday with the threat of the flood waters averted and the cattle moved to higher ground, Beale bounded lithely up the stairs. He and Peta had a date with destiny, and he wasn't willing to put it off any longer. He wanted his wife back. These past two weeks had been a nightmare for the both of them. When he thought of the jealous tantrums he'd subjected Peta to, he felt a complete bastard. He hoped she'd give him the chance to apologise for his boorish behaviour. Also, he needed to set the record straight about Marla and the embrace that Peta had witnessed.

He'd virtually been in a state of shock, his mind reeling from the false accusations that Marla had made towards Peta. Marla had then flung herself into his arms and he had momentarily held her to save himself from overbalancing, but that had been the extent of it. He realised she must have heard Peta coming back into the room and had taken the opportunity to discredit him in Peta's eyes. How could Peta think he had feelings for that detestable woman? It had been all he could do to put up with her for as long as he did. Beale desperately hoped Nelson had been correct about Peta's loving feelings towards himself. It cheered him immensely to think that she loved him.

Jolly usually came bounding out to meet him every afternoon when he arrived home, but today an eerie silence greeted him, which chilled him to the bone, sending ominous shivers up and down the length of his spine. A quick walk through the homestead confirmed his worst fears, Peta wasn't here. His stomach contracted with nervous apprehension as he thought of the alternatives to her whereabouts.

Leaving with Nelson topped the list, and his mind didn't delve into any further explanations about where his wife could be. She had left him! The words rang out ominously in his brain, clearing it of any other conscious thought.

Beale sat down, suddenly weary beyond belief as he contemplated what his next move should be.

Peta walked steadily through the gathering darkness, wanting to get home as soon as possible. She was still not courageous enough to be wandering around the property in the dead of night. She could hear the ominous sounds of small animals all around her as they started their nocturnal foraging, and fervently hoped that she didn't come across any that would pose a threat to her.

She could feel the hairs on the back of her neck prickling her as she nervously looked at the darkening landscape. Everything looked so different of a night-time, but she was sure of her bearings and walked resolutely on. Her persistence was rewarded when a few minutes later she made out the lights of the homestead glowing softly in the distance, standing out like a beacon welcoming her home.

Peta was proud of her achievements, being able to find her way home meant she was becoming accustomed to the environment around her. She hoped Beale would be equally proud of her when she told him of her navigating skills. *That is, if he doesn't kill me first for being so late. He's probably worried sick and on the verge of sending the men out to find me, if he hasn't set up a full scale search already.*

Guilt coursed through her as she thought of Beale wondering where she was. It never entered her mind that he might think she had left with Nelson earlier in the day. *Please let him listen to me*, she prayed to the starlit heavens above. *Surely we can sit down like two mature adults and listen to each other's point of view without falling into an argument.* They hadn't been on the best of terms lately, that was true, but she was determined to make him listen to her before he cast her aside for the beautiful Marla.

By the time she arrived home, Peta had convinced herself that Beale wouldn't want to listen to anything she had to tell him. Last night's fiasco with Nelson had probably left him thinking that she loved his friend. She would think the same thing if she saw Marla in his arms. Hell, she had seen Marla in his arms. She was determined to convince him that her love for Nelson was like that of a brother and not even remotely near to the overpowering love she felt for him. Nelson was her confidante, the only person she had left in the world to whom she could pour out her heart.

Peta found Beale asleep on the spare bed in the sleepout. He was fully dressed and beside him on the floor was a partially empty bottle of Scotch whisky. Her heart went out to him, and she feasted her eyes lovingly down the length of his lanky frame. In sleep, the events of the past few days had disappeared, and he seemed to be almost vulnerable. She noticed tenderly that he needed a shave. The black stubble covering his face and neck gave him a certain strength, even in sleep. Peta could detect a few smatterings of gray amongst the dark shadow. She wished longingly she could bend down to kiss the mouth he offered so invitingly to her in sleep. He stirred her emotions like no other man ever had. Didn't the silly blockhead know she loved him with all of her heart and soul? She smiled at the euphemism she had used in thinking about him. But if the shoe fits, she told herself simply.

Squaring her shoulders in a businesslike manner, Peta forced her mind back to the matter at hand. If she didn't try to fix this terrible mistake that was yawning between them like a great chasm, she would never be able to kiss those wonderfully sexy lips again.

Going over the advice in her mind that Nelson had given her about declaring her love for him, Peta stepped uncertainly forward towards the bed. Now was going to be the time to get everything out into the open between them before anything else marred the path they had promised to tred together.

Biting her lip, Peta hesitated, thinking that maybe she was being too hasty in her decision to tell Beale she loved him. What if Nelson was mistaken, and he didn't love her? It would just be like Nelson to push her forward like this into a situation where even friendship would be beyond them if his assumptions proved to be wrong.

Maybe I should just accept the original terms of our marriage and give in, taking whatever crumbs he chooses to throw me. But Peta knew instinctively that she couldn't accept second best, especially if that meant standing in line with a bunch of other women.

She could accept the fact that he didn't love her, if she was forced to, because he hadn't made her any promises that love would magically appear out of the blue when he'd asked her to be his wife, but I need to know that I can count on his honesty and his integrity to honour our marriage vows.

The one thing about which Peta was adamant was that she wouldn't accept infidelity in their marriage. If Beale felt the need to entertain other women, then he'd have to forfeit their relationship, for she wasn't going to become another notch in his belt.

Peta's moment of truth had arrived and, taking a deep breath to steady herself, she sat down on the bed next to Beale.

"Beale," she shook his shoulder gently to wake him up, "Beale, can I tell you something?"

He stirred and slowly opened his eyes, looking up at her as if in a dream.

"Mmm," he answered groggily, trying to wake up. Was it really Peta, or was he dreaming?

Taking another deep breath to settle the fluttering that had assembled in the pit of her stomach, Peta told him, "I love you, Beale. I always have, since before we were married. Please don't mind, I couldn't help myself."

Peta felt his body go rigid as he lay on the bed, but he remained silent, making her believe he was angry at her admission. Had she complicated things for him by declaring her love for him? Would he feel he had to stay married to her out of a sense of chivalry, but she was sure that Marla wouldn't allow it?

"Please don't be mad. I couldn't help falling in love with you," she repeated, close to tears, but she didn't regret sharing her greatest secret with the one person she loved most in the world.

Beale turned away from her then, reaching over to turn on the bedside lamp. Turning back to her, he casually rolled himself up on to an elbow so he could see her clearly. He wanted to see her face.

"You love me!" He forced the words out. His heart felt like it was going to explode inside his chest.

Peta nodded tearfully as she gazed down at him from where she was sitting on the side of the bed. He certainly didn't appear to be mad. If she'd had to pick an emotion to explain the look he was sending her, she would have chosen shock. He seemed to be fighting an emotional battle with himself and Peta could see the shock on his face was being replaced with another emotion. His face held a joy that she hadn't seen before, and a slow smile spread across his handsome features as he gazed tenderly up at her. Peta's heart had begun to thud heavily in her chest as she dared to hope. Was it possible that he loved her too? How sweet that would be.

"Beale?" she questioned, hopefully needing to know if her heart's desire had indeed been given to her. Tentatively, at first, she reached out with trembling fingers to touch his mouth, feeling him tremble beneath her gentle touch.

Placing his hand gently over hers, he stilled her roving fingers, bringing them down to his chest, where he held them firmly against his swiftly beating heart.

After what seemed like an eternity of waiting, he answered her. "Yes, I love you. I always have, since before we were married." His words rang in her ears, filling her heart with joy and a sweet promise. They were her words, and he had recited them back to her.

"Oh, Beale," she cried as happiness flooded her entire being. "We've both been so stupid, but I was scared to tell you. Love wasn't a part of our agreement, and I thought that if you found out I loved you, it would complicate matters. There have been so many times when I've wanted to tell you how I felt."

"That's how I felt. It feels so good to be able to tell you how much I love you, not to be afraid that I might accidentally blurt out my true feelings when we made love. I've had to stop myself so many times. Do you know how lousy I've felt that I couldn't tell my wife that I loved her?" He pulled her down on to the bed beside him until the length of her was cushioned against him and buried his face into the long silky strands of her hair, breathing in deeply the essence of her.

"Tell me now," she asked seductively, pulling him closer still to her burning body.

Beale told her many times during the night that he loved her, that he would always need her, that she meant everything to him. He knew how corny he sounded, but he meant every word and he needed Peta to know that these feelings came from the very depths of his heart.

Next morning as they lay happily entwined in each other's arms, Peta told him about the cave and the journals she had found containing the information about Kathleen Jacobs.

Beale was dumbfounded. "You crawled inside a cave through thorn bushes!"

Beale found this to be amazing for just the other night she'd run screaming out of the bathroom because a small frill necked lizard had taken refuge under the bathtub.

"Yes. I had to make sure Jolly was alright."

"Why didn't you tell me?"

"I wanted to, but when I got home Marla was here and you seemed so pleased to see her. I guess I was jealous of her," she finished lamely.

"Pleased! I was panic-stricken! I guess was trying to make you jealous, but it backfired on me big time. I never want to go through that again as long as I live," Beale confessed.

"You can say that again. I didn't think it was possible to be that miserable," Peta told him truthfully. "Why were you trying to make me jealous?"

"It all stems from the conversation I had with mum the night she wanted to see me. She said you loved me. And rather than ask you straight out, like an idiot, I thought if you saw me interacting with Marla, you might show your true feelings. Tell me you loved me, but you didn't. So I was more confused than ever. I didn't believe her."

Peta still didn't understand, and threw him a confused look, so Beale continued with his explanation.

"Mum told me about Marla's impending visit, but she also told me something concerning dad's will that I wasn't aware of. Apparently, my father signed the power-of-attorney over to my mother in case he passed first. She said she was curious to see what I'd do about the proviso in the will, saying I'd have to marry before I turned thirty-five. She wondered how far I'd go to keep Blackrock. She also said that if I was stupid enough to marry Marla, she would have enforced dad's will, but as soon as she met you, she knew we were meant to be together."

Peta knew her mouth must be gaping as she took all of this additional information in. Even after hearing all of this extra information, Peta had to ask. "Has Marla been here in the last twelve months, Beale."

"Once or twice. She doesn't like it here. She said it's too rural for her, that she prefers the city lights."

"So why did you keep seeing her?" Peta wanted to know.

"She'd contact me. I hadn't seen her for ages before that time we ran into you at the movies. She said she saw me in town. I agreed to take her out," he hesitated momentarily before taking a deep breath to continue, "I was miffed at you, so I agreed."

"At me! Why? What did I do?" Peta dredged her memory, thinking back to the last time she'd seen him before the fire.

"I was going to ask you out when I picked up the craft stuff for mum. As a thank you, but you got a phone call from someone. You looked so happy, so looking forward to seeing whoever it was. I didn't know who it was. I thought it must be a boyfriend. Anyway, when she phoned me I said okay. The best part of that night was running into you. The funny thing is, I saw Nelson before I went to the movies."

"Oh, Beale, that call was from Nelson. He'd call in to see me whenever he came through Rockhampton. Ah, so it was you he had to see. Otherwise he'd have been at the movies with me." Peta explained to him, but she had to ask this next question, she had to know, "Did you sleep with her?"

"Not that night," Beale told her, hating that she felt she had to ask.

Although this piece of news was a plus, Peta hated that Beale had previously had sex with that horrible woman. How could he! She had to remind herself that he had a life

The Grazier's Proposal

before she met him. He'd been fancy free, able to come and go as he pleased.

He continued, wanting to change the conversation back to them, "Mum adores you. She said we make the perfect match. Trust me, she would have stepped in if she thought we wouldn't make a go of it."

"Do you think she guessed about our arrangement? It certainly sounds like she did," Peta asked him. How could she face Nancy when the other woman thought their marriage was a sham?

"Perhaps, but that's something she'll keep to herself, but this I do know, she didn't like Marla," seeing Peta's face starting to frown, he quickly added, "Either do I so you can put your mind at rest on that score. I love you. God, it feels so good to be able to tell you. I love you," he told her, then repeated again. "I love you, I love you, I love you."

"I thought you'd asked the men to take me out with them when they went to Deadman's Gorge so you could spend time with Marla." Just the thought of the pain she'd suffered was enough to crease her face up in remembered torment.

Beale tenderly kissed the creases away from her forehead. "Good lord, no. I wanted her off the place, and the sooner the better. I dropped her off so she could catch the mail plane back to Rocky and told her never to return because she wasn't welcome. As for the men siding with me, you've got to be kidding. We nearly came to blows." At her look of total disbelief, he continued, "Honest! They called me a jackass." Actually, they'd been more explicit, but he wasn't going to repeat what he'd really been called, "I nearly had a mass walkout on my hands. They took you with them because they wanted to protect you. They're like a flock of mother hens about you. Heaven help me if we ever argue again. My life won't be worth the price of a bullet."

"Oh, how sweet," Peta crooned. Her heart went out to the men as she recalled how incredibly kind they'd been to her throughout the day.

Peta took Beale to the cave and together they retrieved the journals, bringing them back to the house. He read them with interest, but wasn't as affected as Peta had been.

"Beale," she said when he'd put the last journal down, "Do you want our son to be named Beale after you?"

"What?" he was looking at her with renewed interest. "Does this mean what I think it means?" He had risen out of his chair and was across the room with an economy of strides. He knelt down beside her, a curious grin plastered across his mobile face.

"I think so." she beamed at him. "I took a pregnancy test this morning, and it showed positive. We're going to be parents." Peta was gathered up into his arms and held gently within his firm embrace.

"You're going to make a wonderful mother," he told her in a voice that was full of joyous anticipation; "I promise you I will never again doubt you. I'll even let you ask Nelson to be our child's godfather."

Peta's heart soared with the happiness she was feeling. "That's very kind of you, daddy; I'll keep that in mind."

"Peta," Beale cast serious emerald eyes in her direction, "I want you to know that even before I knew about mum having the final say about dad's will; I seriously thought about giving Blackrock up for you."

Peta couldn't speak because of the lump that had lodged itself in her throat. Her eyes welled up with tears as she looked lovingly across at him. She was in little doubt that he meant every word.

"I wouldn't have let you. You belong here, Beale," she told him, not bothering to fight back her tears, letting them course down her cheeks unheeded, "as surely as Kathleen's Beale belonged here. There will always be a Beale Jacobs living on Blackrock Downs. There's no way you're going to lose your heritage. And when the time comes, you'll pass the reins over to our son."

Beale was overcome with heartfelt emotion as he listened to Peta's words, said with so much conviction that they made him feel proud to be married to her.

"But," she tacked on with a growing confidence while looking at him, wanting conformation for her next words, "if we have a daughter, I'd like to call her Kathleen Isobel."

He merely nodded, not quite able to keep the satisfied smirk off his face. He'd been thinking of Peta and their intended family.

"What?" She didn't think she'd said anything worth laughing at.

"Nothing, just that I love you," he told her simply.

She looked back at him through slightly suspicious eyes before telling him in a voice that was filled with love and happiness, "Nelson's right, you are a blockhead."

He laughed as he gathered her up into his arms and carried her down the hallway to their bedroom. He was going to see that she got plenty of rest, for within her womb she was carrying the next generation, their son, who would one day take his rightful place as the owner of Blackrock Downs.

THE END

About the author

Hi. I'm *Carolyn Pollack*.

I'm an average, mostly stay at home arts and craft/pottery addict. No pets to speak of anymore, but I do feed the wild birds that arrive every morning wanting to be fed. Apparently, I also have a possum that eats the left over bird feed. I retired from full time work in 2017, but I found I missed the clients I worked with within the disability sector, and begged my former employer to allow me to come back to do pottery with them for a few hours a week.

I did this for a while and was perfectly happy with my lot in life – well, almost. My passion for writing has always been festering just below the surface and every now and again it bursts through giving me a jolt in the right direction, which is towards the computer to write down the myriad of ideas that seem to pop randomly into my head. Then, they get embellished and added to the new novel that I've started to write. It's coming along quite nicely.

I have once again started working one day a week for a disability company here in Rockhampton as an art therapy teacher. It keeps me on my toes, but I'm loving it.

At the same time, though, I thought I'd re-edit and re-publish the 4 novels I'd previously written. I've been doing this for the last twelve months. This one, formally known as Sealed With A Kiss has also been given a new title. It is now titled, The Grazier's Proposal. I think it's a much better alternative.

This is the third novel that Pen Author Solutions have done for me. The other two are, A Date With Destiny and Vendetta of Love. They are out and ready to be read.

You can find me on my Instagram page as cjpollack1. Go and have a look. Hopefully, you'll find something interesting to tweak your curiosity and hopefully, perhaps, make you feel you would like to read one of my books. You might even find a podcast that will make you smile, or maybe laugh at me. Only one way to find out, hey.

Anyway, if you have A Grazier's Proposal in front of you, I wish you happy reading.

My Website:
http://carolynjunepollack.com/.

www.ingramcontent.com/pod-product-compliance
Lightning Source LLC
LaVergne TN
LVHW021700060526
838200LV00050B/2440